WILM

KU-012-475

96

Hit and Run

Titles in the Harvestime **Pressure Points** series:

Hit and Run

Liz Priestley

Harvestime

Published in the United Kingdom by:
Harvestime Services Ltd, 12a North Parade, Bradford
West Yorkshire BD1 3HT

Copyright © 1989 Liz Priestley
First published by Harvestime
First printed March 1989

All rights reserved.

No part of this publication may be reproduced or
transmitted, in any form or by any means, electronic
or mechanical, including photocopy, recording or any
information storage and retrieval system, without
permission in writing from the publisher.

British Library Cataloguing in Publication Data

Priestley, Liz
  Hit and run. – (Pressure points series).
  I. Title II. Series
  823'.914 [J]

  ISBN 0-947714-67-7

Typeset in the United Kingdom by:
E. Thompson (Typesetters) Ltd., Bradford BD4 7BG
Printed and bound in the United Kingdom by:
Richard Clay Ltd, Bungay, Suffolk

Contents

To

Uncle Norman and Mrs B.
with love

1

Duff day

As soon as I got up that morning I knew it was going to be a rubbishy day. For a start, I overslept and didn't have time for a shower. You won't understand what a disaster that is unless you've got hair like mine.

The day was confirmed as being D for duff when I discovered that Adam, my four-year-old brother, had scoffed the last of my breakfast cereal. I can't understand what made Mum let him have it – she knows that's the only stuff I can eat in a morning. I had to settle for a packet of crisps and a chocolate milkshake instead.

Mum blasted off about it, but I was already halfway through the crisps before she saw me.

Normally I like to mess about a bit before school, but I knew I wouldn't have time. So I shoved my feet in my shoes without unfastening the laces and rubbed toothpaste on my teeth with my finger. Well, why not? All Mum checks up on is the minty smell, and I can always give them a good do later.

Then I got down to the serious business of sorting out this bird's-nest I've got instead of hair.

All the kids at school laugh at my hair, but I can tell you it's no joke – not when you're the one it's attached to! It's OK if I can wash it every day and force it all to go in the same direction while it's wet. But if the system fails – like it did this morning – it looks like a mousey-coloured haystack, with bits sticking out in all directions.

Dad's hair's the same, but he keeps it under control with his Parkhurst Prison haircut – but I'm blowed if I'll go that far. I've got my pride.

Grabbing a comb and the plastic spray-gun Mum uses for the ironing, I headed hotfoot for the mirror in the hall, and it was there that Dad found me when he came downstairs.

'What in heaven's name are you doing, Darrel?' he demanded, ducking to avoid the cascade of water from the spray. 'You're wetting the wallpaper.'

'Sorry, Dad,' I muttered abstractedly. 'Everything's gone wrong this morning, and I can't get my hair out of haystack mode.' I sprayed again – a bit more gently this time – and dragged the comb through the droplets on my head.

'It beats me why you don't just have it cut short like I do,' said Dad, tucking the newspaper under his arm and going into the kitchen. 'It's no bother at all like this.'

'You must be joking,' I thought, tugging at the wet straw. 'I'm not *that* desperate!' A tooth broke off the comb and fell on the carpet. 'On the other hand, I might just consider it.'

'Oh, by the way,' said Dad, turning back, 'don't arrange anything for after school. Mum and I have something we want to talk to you about.'

My heart dropped into my boots.

I knew it. Total confirmation of the day ahead being a complete wash-out. Dad had finally made the decision that was going to change our lives.

'Great timing, Dad,' I muttered, scowling savagely at my scruffy reflection. I looked awful. 'Daz Chadwick,' I said, 'you're a walking disaster.'

Throwing down the comb, I abandoned the fight with my pestiferous mop and followed Dad into the kitchen.

Mum was cleaning off the side of Adam's head, which he'd accidentally skimmed with toast and honey. Dad was reading the paper and Gyles Brandreth was showing off another of his yucky sweaters on breakfast TV. (Mum thinks they're great – isn't that just typical?) Everything looked the same as usual, but I knew things were on the point of changing for ever.

'What's this talk going to be about, Dad?'

'Not now, Darrel. I'll tell you tonight when we've got more time. Better get a move on, son, or you'll be late.' He obviously wasn't letting anything go, so I grabbed my bag and headed for the door.

'See you after school, kid,' I said, ruffling the dry side of Adam's blond hair as I passed. He grinned at me through his sticky little specs, jaws still firmly cemented together with toast and honey.

'See you, Mum.' I gave her a quick peck on the cheek. OK, so it's uncool. But my mum's all right, and I know she likes it, so I do it. After that, I barely had time to grab my bike from the garage and race to school before the bell rang.

Being late in the morning can put you out for the whole day. I'd forgotten my homework, but that wasn't too drastic 'cos Ranjit let me copy his during break. The worst was that I'd also forgotten my games kit, so I got a blasting from Mr Carter, missed the class soccer match and was given a load of extra maths.

But mostly it was the worry about Dad's little talk that was the problem – I just couldn't get my brain into gear at all, so I had all sorts of aggro from the teachers for not concentrating. My mind just kept going over everything that had happened at home over the last few months.

Things had been pretty mixed up for us since Hadley's

Mill closed and Dad was made redundant. He'd worked there for umpteen years – long before I was born. But over the last few years nearly all the heavy industry in the area – engineering and suchlike – had gone. Hadley's was the only one left, so when it closed down it was as though the town of Newton Bridge just rolled over and died.

There'd been rumours of redundancies for ages, and it was all pretty unsettling, so when news of the shut-down finally came through it actually made life easier for a while. At least we knew where we were.

I remember redundancy day really well – Dad took me off fishing so that we could have a man-to-man chat about everything. We sat on the bank of the river in our waterproofs, eating sandwiches and discussing what redundancy was really going to mean to us. Dad's no quitter – he'd already written to every engineering firm within thirty miles.

'I'm going to try the lot and see what happens,' he'd said optimistically. 'It's early days yet. Pass us that flask of soup, Darrel. If nothing comes up we'll think again.'

'Dad,' I'd asked apprehensively, 'we won't have to leave our house, will we?' I'd just got my room exactly how I wanted it, so there was no way I was going to move. His answer wasn't totally reassuring.

'No problem there,' he'd said, passing me a cup of Mum's home-made soup. 'Not for a bit anyway. But we've got to keep an open mind about it.'

I'd watched the river slide gently past as I sipped the hot soup. Lentil and tomato – great! We'd had a lot of home-made stuff since Dad had been out of work 'cos Mum reckoned it was cheaper to make your own stuff than buy it. But I think the taste's a massive improvement, too.

'Move? No way!' I'd thought, deliberately closing my mind to the idea. If we moved, it'd be over my dead body!

2

Maggots and money

The first few months of Dad's redundancy were great. He was always around during the day, and we went all over the place – fishing, bowling, visiting museums and exhibitions, even doing jobs on the house together. It was ace!

After a while nobody mentioned getting a new job very much because, although Dad was applying for anything that came up, he never got an interview – some firms never even replied to his letters.

'There's hundreds of people writing for these jobs,' he explained. 'I can understand companies not replying – it would cost them a fortune in postage if they did.'

Compared to some other families we had quite a cushy number – Dad had masses of redundancy pay 'cos he'd worked for Hadley's for so long, and Mum still had her job packing 'special offers' while Adam was at nursery.

But we had to cut back on our spending because the future was so uncertain and our money wouldn't last for ever. Dad stopped going for a pint in the evening, I had a cut in pocket-money and Mum was making meals out of stuff that normally got sent round for next-door's dog.

By July, though, Dad's joke about Bovril sandwiches being the only meat in his diet was turning into reality,

and he started getting restless. The first inkling we had of
what was in his mind came one Saturday lunchtime.

'I forgot to tell you, Sylvia,' he'd said, reaching across
the table for the cheese. 'I saw Jim Ormerod last night,
and he says Harry Fielding and his wife have gone to
Morecambe.'

Mum was pouring tea and making sure Adam didn't
start on the jam before he'd had something 'nutritious' –
she was into health food by this time.

'That's nice,' she observed, passing round the mugs.
'I could do with a few days away myself.'

'No, love. I mean G-O-N-E. Packed up, sold the house
– *gone*. They've bought a little business with his
redundancy money – a newsagent's I think – and it looks
like they're there for good.'

'How could they afford to buy a shop?' said Mum. 'He
wasn't at Hadley's any longer than you, and he didn't have
such a good job, either.'

'They sold the house, remember. Jim says they live in
a flat above the shop.'

'I wonder how his wife likes that,' she remarked, cutting
some more bread. 'I've never fancied living in a flat.'

'You wouldn't have to stay there for ever, would you?'
Dad leaned forward earnestly. 'Just long enough to get the
business on its feet, then we could buy a house and . . . .'

Up to that point I'd been more or less ignoring the
conversation, but when Dad said 'we' all my warning bells
rang.

'Who's this "we" you're talking about?' asked Mum
warily.

'Good question, Mum!' I thought, sitting up and taking
notice. Dad looked guilty.

'I didn't mean to mention it now, really. I was going
to do my homework on it and then talk to you when I'd
got all the facts.' He paused and then rushed on, 'But it

seems to me that the chances of finding another job round here are nil. We might as well sell up like the Fieldings and start again somewhere else.'

'I know it'll mean a big change,' he said quickly, seeing our horrified faces. 'But I think we've got to face facts and consider some alternatives. We can't go on for ever like this.'

Hearing all that had thrown me for the rest of the day. I hadn't bothered going to football practice, but just lay on my bed boggling about the awful prospect of leaving Newton Bridge. The thought of moving house was bad enough – but moving town was something else!

Mum and Dad never mentioned it again when I was around – probably because I'd thrown a wobbler that lunchtime and said that if they went they'd have to go without me. I knew Mum hated the idea, too, but they were obviously still looking into it 'cos I kept finding estate agent's leaflets all over the house.

Then, one Sunday in summer, it had surfaced again when we were at Grandma's for tea.

Grandma Middleton lived just round the corner from our house in a specially designed old person's bungalow packed full of her interesting bits and pieces. For a year or two after Grandpa's death she'd been OK, but then her eyesight had gone right down the tubes with some sort of disease – glau-something, the specialist had said.

Mum wasn't too happy about her being alone – but since she'd wanted to stay there, and because it was only round the corner, we'd just fixed her up with a cordless telephone and made sure we called in a lot.

That particular Sunday me and Adam had been outside her house playing cricket – at least, we were until Adam clouted me on the knuckles with the bat. You may laugh, but I was rolling about in agony. The little ratbag had drawn blood!

He was laughing fit to burst, so to avoid wringing his neck I hobbled into the house, and it was while I was in the bathroom nursing and cursing that I caught part of a conversation in the kitchen that made my stomach turn over.

'I can't see any other way round it, Mother,' Mum was saying, her words floating clearly through the thin wall. 'I don't want to move away either, but it looks as though there's nothing else we can do. But I'd never have a moment's peace if you were here on your own. You just couldn't manage! Brian and I have talked it over: we want you to come with us.'

I sat on the edge of the bath with my heart in my boots. It looked almost certain that we were going to leave Newton Bridge – but where on earth were we going?

Grandma's voice filtered through, wobbly with distress. 'I don't know what to think, Sylvia. I wish your father was still here – he always made the decisions. What if you get sick of me? It's not easy having an old person living with you.'

Mum tutted loudly.

'No, I'm serious. And what about all my things?'

There was a pause.

'Our family's always lived in the West Riding. I don't know if I could settle anywhere else.'

'Same here, Grandma,' I thought, pressing my ear to the cold wall to catch the words. Me and Grandma think that West Yorkshire – she calls it by it's old name, the West Riding – is the only place to live.

'Be reasonable, Mother. Frinsham's hardly the end of the world – it's still in Yorkshire, for heaven's sake!'

So that was it. Frinsham! Dad was thinking of dragging us off to Frinsham. I could hardly believe it – and I knew I'd never forgive him if he went through with it.

Teatime had been a real pain. Everybody sat around

pretending to eat and pushing ham and salad from one side of their plates to the other.

Not that that's anything new. Ham and salad must be the world's most boring meal, and that's what Grandma always gave us. The only time I enjoyed it was when Mum found half a maggot in her lettuce. The interesting bit – for us, not Mum – was not being able to find the other half! Mum turned green and rushed off to the toilet. She's been neurotic about salad ever since.

No-one knew I'd been listening in the bathroom, so they all thought I was sulking about my injured hand. Adam was the only one unaffected. He just set about his food like Pac-Man – maggots or no maggots. It was disgusting.

Next day at school I'd felt dead off-colour about everything, and ended up at the end of the morning with two detentions and some extra French. That really brassed me off 'cos I hate French.

Those days, the only thing that seemed to cheer me up was spending money. Sometimes I'd blow a whole week's pocket-money and my paper-round wage in one day, usually on sweets and comics – just stupid stuff. That dinnertime was one of those times, and I persuaded Dave and Ranjit to sneak out of school with me to go to the shops.

After spending a bomb on crisps and chocolate I felt better. Then I realised I'd spent my swimming money for that night, which meant increasing my secret borrowings from Mum's twenty-pence coin collection when I got home. I didn't want to admit it, but this was getting to be a problem.

Mum never saw me touch her twenty-pence tin, and I always tried to replace the money straightaway – not that she'd have noticed if I hadn't, 'cos she never counted it – but I'd taken quite a bit that month. Far more than I was able to put back.

'It's for a rainy day,' Mum would say as she dropped

a coin through the hole in the lid. Well, I was having a lot of 'rainy days' just then, so if I felt a bit nervous of her finding out I consoled myself with the thought that I'd only borrowed it. Paying it back would be easy when I started getting a decent amount of pocket-money again.

Anyway, all that was just minor hassle – the real problem was what Mum had been saying about Frinsham, so on the way back into school I'd given Dave and Ranjit a blow-by-blow account of what I'd heard in Grandma's bathroom.

If I was expecting sympathy, I was disappointed – in fact, I ended up dead narked. Best pals? Huh! I thought they'd be devastated to lose me – but *no*.

'You lucky geezer, Chadwick!' said Dave, as we dodged through the gap in the wire and strolled innocently back up the field. 'I'd give my right arm to live at the seaside!'

'Yeah! We'll come over and stay with you,' echoed Ranjit.

'Well, thank you and good night, faithful friends,' I snapped bitterly. 'I think the idea stinks.'

Dave was quite taken aback. 'What's up with you? It's not that we want you to go – no way! – but Frinsham's a fantastic . . . .'

'That's right,' Ranjit cut in. 'If it was me I'd be dead pleased. I went there on a school trip once – it was great. We went on the beach, along the harbour, up to the . . . .'

'Give it a rest, Ranjit. I don't want to know,' I said rattily. It's depressing when your best pals don't understand. They shuffled about a bit, throwing what-shall-we-do-with-him glances at each other.

'OK, you guys,' I sighed, levering myself off the wall. 'Sorry for being a pain.'

Without being too obvious, I positioned myself for a flying start. 'Last one to the trees – stinks!'

I won, of course. And Dave stank.

Since then I'd just hoped that if I ignored it, it would go away – but now Dad had blown all my hopes to smithereens, and I was looking forward to that night's little talk like he was going to announce the end of the world.

3

Blackmailed!

As it turned out, I needn't have altered my plans for that night 'cos Dad was out till six o'clock – 'seeing a man about a horse', which is Chadwickese for 'mind your own business'. When he turned up it was teatime, and Mum made it very obvious that nothing would be said until Adam had hit the sack.

'Darrel, just get Adam sorted out for me, will you, while I clear the table and make a pot of tea?'

'OK, kid. Follow me,' I said, picking up an armful of toys and heading for the door.

We went upstairs together, and I stood over him while he got his pyjamas on, helping him with the difficult bits. Finally he was dressed – just his teeth and face to do.

'Where's Scrags?' he said, searching the room through little round glasses for his revolting old rag of a blanket.

'You don't need Scrags when you're cleaning your teeth.'

'Yes, I do! First I put my 'jamas on, then I say hello to Scrags, then I clean my teeth.'

I knew from experience that there was no point arguing, so I got down on my hands and knees and searched the bedroom for Scrags, while Adam stood in the middle of the room shouting 'Scraggy! Where a-a-re yo-u-u-u?' I'm glad none of my pals could see us – little brothers are really humiliating.

Eventually I found it. (The rest of my crazy family toe the line and call the thing 'him', but I refuse.) It was stuffed between the bed and the wall. Then I had to stand and watch as Adam struggled to suck his thumb, clean his teeth and hold on to Scrags, all at the same time.

Mum's arrival put a stop to that, and after a minute or two we were able to shut his door and go back downstairs.

The coffee-table was covered with official-looking papers which Dad hurriedly moved to make room for the tea-tray. He shuffled through them nervously, glancing up as Mum and I settled ourselves on the sofa.

'We didn't want to say anything to you until things were more certain,' he said, collecting the papers into two or three untidy piles. 'I know you're not happy about moving away, but your Mum and I thought that if you knew where we were going you might . . . .'

'You told me we wouldn't have to move!' I interrupted accusingly. (Not strictly true, but so what?) 'Don't think you can bribe me with Frinsham. I'm not going anywhere!'

Dad nearly dropped his tea. 'How the heck did you know it was Frinsham?'

'I heard Mum trying to persuade Grandma last weekend – but you'll never get her to leave, either.'

'She wasn't keen, that's true,' admitted Mum, 'but she knows it has to be done, so she's agreed.'

I couldn't believe it! This was a major let-down.

'She's an old lady, Darrel – and nearly blind, too. She had to face the fact that she could never manage without us.'

That was the truth – but, all the same, I felt as if Grandma had been blackmailed, and I said so.

Dad leaned forward and pointed a warning finger at me.

'I don't like the attitude you're taking about this, Darrel. No-one wants to leave – this has been my home all *my* life, too. But if I stay here I could be on social security for ever. We've got to make a move, and the sooner the better. I'm sorry, son, but you've got to get used to the idea.'

Hearing his side of things made me realise that I hadn't really given a thought as to how he would feel, leaving the place he'd lived in for over forty years. We'd always got on well, me and Dad, but I'd been cool towards him for ages – ever since he'd mentioned moving away.

Mum slid close and put her arm round my shoulders. 'Try and be interested, love,' she said, giving me an encouraging squeeze. 'It could be a wonderful place to live.'

'That's right,' echoed Dad. 'You'd have the sea, the coast – all that countryside that we could explore together. And less hills to slog up on your bike.'

I gave in. 'OK, OK. I'll listen.'

Mum and Dad breathed a sigh of relief. But they'd better come up with the goods when we get there!

Dad had spent the afternoon with an accountant, someone to give advice about setting up in business and doing the 'books' – whatever they were – and he was now on the point of signing the contracts to buy a grocer's shop in Frinsham.

'It'll mean us all pulling together for a while,' he explained, passing me the estate agent's leaflet. 'We'll have to put up with a few weeks' inconvenience until the shop's on its feet, but after that . . . .'

'Hang on a minute,' I interrupted, scanning the description of the shop and flat. 'This says "three bedrooms" – that's you two, me and Adam. Where's Grandma sleeping? In the bath?'

Nobody laughed.

'It'll only be for a little while – until we get a house
– but we thought that you and Adam . . . .'

'Aw, Mum! No!'

'Just for a month or six weeks . . . .'

'It's not fair! He's only four, and I'm thirteen.'

It was no good, though. Sharing with Adam was the only
way it could be worked out. My one consolation was that
it would just be for a short time – plus Dad's promise
to explore the coast with me. I sighed.

'All right. When do we go?'

* * *

Just before the fifth of November, me and Adam stood in
the road outside what used to be our house, and watched
brown-coated men put the last of our belongings into the
removal van.

Adam thought it was great until he saw his bed being
carried out. Then he blew a gasket!

There was a mad scramble as everybody, including the
removal men, rushed about looking for Scrags. It turned
out that some idiot had packed it somewhere in the van,
and by the time Dad found it Adam was in a right state
– sobbing and hiccuping, his glasses all steamed up.

We sat on the wall, him clutching Scrags, sucking his
thumb and giving the occasional heaving sob, and me
looking at the house and wondering what it was going to
be like living in a flat in a new town and not knowing
anybody.

'Well, that's that,' said Mum, looking far from cheerful.
'Dad's just going to load up Grandma's stuff and then
we're on our way.'

She put her arm round us both, and I got the impression
that she was pretty choked up. 'Dad's going to travel in
the van, so we might as well set off now in the car.'

'What 'bout Grandma?' asked Adam.

'She's going to stay with Auntie Mary for a day or two, so that we can get her room nice for her.'

I had to have one more look round before we went, so I left Mum strapping Adam into his seat-belt and saying goodbye to the neighbours, and went back into the house. All the rooms echoed, and my footsteps sounded like thunder in the empty hall. I felt like a stranger, even though the last of our things had been carried out only minutes before.

Leaping up the stairs two at a time, I clumped across the uncarpeted landing to my bedroom. The only evidence left that it had ever been mine were the lighter patches on the wall where my posters had been, and the telltale streak down the wallpaper where I'd spilled drinking-chocolate.

With a lump in my throat I turned and went back down the stairs, through the empty dining-room and kitchen and out into the garden. It was pretty muddy now, and I could still see clearly where we'd worn the grass away playing cricket during the summer. There wasn't going to be a garden at our new place.

Mum was shouting from the car, so I shut all the doors again, locked up and went out to her.

I'd decided I wasn't going to look back when we left, in case it got to me. But Dave and Ranjit blew it by turning up on their bikes just as we set off, riding alongside us for as long as they could.

Just when I was about to really lose my cool and bawl like a baby, Mum put her foot down and left them far behind, driving out of our road and our town for the last time.

4

Deadly boring

Moving into the flat was chaotic. We'd got rid of tons of stuff before we left Newton Bridge, but there was still far too much for such a small flat – especially with all Grandma's gear as well. The place looked like a warehouse.

'If your father says "only temporary" in that jolly voice once more . . .' muttered Mum between clenched teeth, as Dad and the removal men piled more and more furniture and boxes into the cramped space. She was up to her eyes in newspaper and tea-chests, and Adam was obviously in everybody's way, so I volunteered to take him for a walk.

Mum was really grateful. 'Thanks, love, that's a real help,' she said in relieved tones.

In actual fact, my intentions weren't quite that noble. The truth was that I didn't want to stay in that poky hole, so I was in a guilty grump as we fought our way past all the boxes and out into the street.

'Which way shall we go, kid?' I asked, not really caring two hoots – wherever we went in this town was going to be a drag.

Adam examined the alternatives. Looking to the right, all we could see were houses, but left, down Albert Road, he caught a glimpse in the distance of a high wall and trees.

'Can we go to that par   I shrugged unenthusiastically.

'Sure.'

It felt odd, him trotting quietly beside me like that, holding tight to my hand. Usually it's more like python-wrestling, 'cos he spends the whole time struggling to escape and leap under a bus.

I gazed down at the top of his head. He has a way of looking very small when he's unhappy, and it was written all over him now.

'You OK, Adam?'

'Y-e-es,' he quavered doubtfully. 'But when are we going back to our real house?'

Looking at his worried face, I just didn't know what to say. Why does he always wait and ask *me* these tricky questions?

'Dad must have been off his trolley to bring us here,' I brooded. In Newton Bridge we'd lived on a decent new estate, but this place was prehistoric. The street names gave it away – Victoria Terrace, Albert Road, Prospect Street – every one of them lined with rows of narrow, yellow-brick Victorian terraced houses with postage-stamp gardens.

Living here would be the pits.

'Still,' I thought, standing on the kerb facing the high wall and iron gates, 'if this park's OK, it might be reduced from Mega- to Super-drag.'

I was so busy watching for traffic that Adam's sudden bid for freedom caught me unprepared. Wrenching his hand out of mine, he leapt forward with a whoop of excitement and raced for the gate.

'Hey!' I yelled, sprinting after him. 'Come back!'

You've really got to watch this kid – he can be up to the eyes in filth faster than you can blink. Once, he'd only gone two hundred metres from the car when he measured his length in a cowpat – a neck-to-toe job! Then he just stood there in his birthday suit waving to the trains while

Dad rushed back to the car for clean clothes.

This time I needn't have worried. Leaping through the gate a few seconds later I nearly fell over him, bolted to the ground in front of a huge marble angel. It gazed sightlessly down, its hands streaked with green algae and with several fingers missing, reaching to us over a pot of very dead flowers. This place wasn't a park at all – it was a massive, ancient cemetery.

The gaunt trees and bushes stood like silent mourners behind the rows of elaborate granite and marble gravestones – some of them the size of a mini-bus. It spread in every direction – long avenues disappearing into silent, hidden valleys through dark tunnels of trees.

What a place! Standing there looking at it in the fading daylight really gave me the creeps. After all, I knew quite a bit about these places from the books Kev Watson used to bring into school back in Newton Bridge.

Adam dragged his eyes reluctantly away from the cold, marble face.

'Where's the swings?'

The last thing I wanted to do was hang around there and explain, so I didn't bother answering – just marched him back through the gate and along the pavement at a fast clip, looking round now and again to make sure we were alone.

He protested every step of the way, until eventually I got sick of it and fetched him a quick swipe across his bobble hat – a move I instantly regretted as the wail rose to a shriek.

A frantic search in my anorak pocket produced a furry sweet – pretty yucky, really, but it reduced the decibels to a snivel.

Following the curve of the road we passed a monumental mason's yard, its showroom filled with headstones – black, white, and that awful salmon-pink that looks like cheap cat-food. Then there were several large houses with brass nameplates – a doctor's, an osteo-something and a few others – and a church.

The houses were bigger here, but still boringly Victorian – and they didn't have real gardens. Everything was built of the same tasteless yellow brick – even the church.

We'd walked in a big circle, and now stood on the corner of Victoria Terrace, undecided what to do next. Adam was complaining about the cold and the lack of swings and said he wanted to go back to Mum. I knew we'd be as popular in the flat as a snake in a sleeping-bag, but what else could I do?

We dragged out a bit more time by looking into people's front rooms on the way back, but he wasn't amused. I wanted to stop and see the posters in the video shop window, but Adam had really had enough and by the time we got back to the shop he was complaining at maximum volume.

If anything, things were worse than when we'd left. Gear was piled up in massive heaps everywhere, Dad was nowhere to be seen, and the men were still bringing stuff in.

Mum emerged, dirty and hot, from behind a stack of boxes. Her blonde hair, neatly tied in a pony-tail at the start, now hung round her ears in scruffy hanks. She brushed it angrily out of her eyes, giving me a scorching look as Adam started whingeing about how I'd hit him and dragged him away from the 'funny park'.

'Darrel,' she hissed. 'What're you playing at, for Pete's sake? I thought you were getting him out of the way.'

I was staggered by the injustice of it all.

'We've been out for ages,' I protested. 'Adam was freezing so we had to come back. Besides,' I glowered at her over the top of the junk, 'the "funny park", as he calls it, is a cemetery – and that just about sums up the entertainment in this place. They probably all died of

boredom – just like I'm going to.'

'Don't be silly – and don't talk to me in that tone!' she snapped. 'There's a bed made up in your room, so take Adam up there and get some toys for him. Then find out where your dad is – he's just disappeared and left me to sort all this out.'

Adam cheered up quite a bit when he found his bed in the attic. It wasn't a bad room really, but I'd already decided that this whole move was going to be rubbish – so, even though we had the biggest room, I pointed out to Mum that I could only stand up in half of it because of the sloping roof.

She just snorted and walked off. OK, so maybe she did have her own gripes and worries, but it just proved that nobody gave a hoot what I thought about anything.

Leaving Adam with Scrags and He-man, I went off in search of Dad, fighting my way through the mountains of junk like Indiana Jones, but he was nowhere to be found. Noises came from the yard, but it was only Mum stacking empty crates outside – so that just left the shop.

The door was open and I hovered there, reluctant to go in 'cos it was getting dark and I didn't know where the lights were. I could make out the square of glass in the shop door, but the big windows were covered with shelves and adverts that blocked out what was left of the daylight. The place was a dim cave of half-seen, humpy shapes.

'Dad,' I bawled into the murk. 'Da-a-a-a-d!'

I was just giving up and turning away when a horrible sound made my blood run cold and my hair stand on end – an eerie sort of screeching moan, followed by a thud and heavy, hollow steps.

You can laugh if you like, but you weren't there. I was rooted to the spot. Like I said, I knew all about this sort of thing from Kev's books.

Ghostly light filtered up behind the counter, bringing

with it an evil, musty stench. Then a grotesque figure slowly rose – hunchbacked and holding what looked like a body.

My heart was pounding and I was just about to faint when the figure spoke.

'Some idiot's taken out all the light bulbs down here,' said Dad, coming up through the cellar trap-door like Blackpool Tower Organ. 'Would you credit it! And they've left these sacks of spuds rotting down there, too.'

He moved the torch from the top of the reeking sack where it had been shining right up his nose, creating a really weird effect.

'Remind me to oil the hinges on that trap-door.'

5

Jackson's Bay

'A few days of chaos, then it's plain sailing,' said Dad cheerfully as we sat among the boxes eating fish and chips that first night.

His scary rise from the cellar had actually given us all a well-deserved laugh. Mum said she was sorry for being snappy, and I was feeling generally more hopeful about things. But I needn't have bothered. All Dad's cheerful talk turned out to be a load of rubbish. Things got worse, not better.

For a start, Grandma arrived long before things were sorted out. We still had piles of stuff all over the place – mostly in her room – so we had to shift all the boxes out and find somewhere else to put them. Me and Adam got quite a few in our room, but the rest were stacked on the stairs – and they stayed there for weeks.

Mum got really snappy about it. 'I reckon these stairs are the nearest I'm going to get to shelves in this place,' she complained. 'One of us'll have to break a leg over this lot before your dad'll do something about it.'

She could have saved her breath – Dad never even heard her 'cos he was too busy doing the rotten books. We hardly saw him – well, not properly. He was always at the wholesaler's or doing something in the shop – filling shelves or painting or sorting out the cellar. And when he *was* with us he had his head buried in those rotten account books.

Sometimes he even ate his meals in the shop. And as for buying another house and exploring the countryside – well, that was just a joke. Mum blew her stack regularly – especially when she found stuff from the wholesaler's joining the other gear on the stairs.

'As if we hadn't got enough in here already, without crates of beans and loo-rolls!' she exploded. 'You've been promising to sort it out for more than three months. I'm fed up with it!'

'Mmm? What?' murmured Dad absently, head still buried in the account books.

'You haven't heard a word I've been saying, have you?'

'Mmm?' he repeated, still not listening.

Mum glared at him, hands on hips, stiff with annoyance.

Suddenly he looked up, a worried frown creasing his forehead. 'I can't understand it, Sylvia. Either old Jarvis was cooking the books, or I'm doing something drastically wrong.'

'What's "cooking the books"?' I asked, puzzled.

'What your dad means,' snapped Mum, 'is that he thinks Mr Jarvis, who sold us the business, was on the fiddle . . . .'

'I never said that!'

'. . . and that he made the shop sound better than it was, so that your Dad would pay more money for it.'

'That's not what I meant. But,' he shuffled through the pile of receipts, 'I'm having to spend a fortune on new stock. Most of that stuff in the cellar had to go. It was old enough to have come out of the ark. We couldn't sell it – folks could have died of food poisoning. But I just seem to be pouring money into the shop, and getting hardly anything out.'

You could say that again! My pocket-money had already been a casualty of his spending cuts, and there were no signs of improvement. 'Tightening our belts' he called it. 'Only temporary, of course'. Yeah, just like everything else.

The only person who never complained was Grandma. It must have been really hard for her, feeling that she was always in the way. Nobody said anything straight out, but me and Adam griped all the time about having to share a room, and Mum moaned on about being 'stuck inside these four walls looking after people'.

Mum had enjoyed her part-time job in Newton Bridge, and she was missing it. Me, I missed the money she earned – it used to pay for my trips out and my clothes.

'How can I go out when the place is like this?' she'd witter on. 'Mother can't even see to find her way to the toilet without falling over something – I can't possibly leave her.'

As for me – just sharing the attic with Adam was a nightmare. For a start, I wasn't allowed up there after seven o'clock because he was in bed, so I had to stay in the sitting-room all evening watching daft TV game-shows and soaps – putrid stuff! – 'cos Mum said Grandma liked them.

'Let Darrel watch his programmes, Sylvia,' Grandma would say. But Mum's reply was always: 'It's all right, Mother. It does him good not to get his own way all the time.'

That wasn't fair, but Mum was getting rattier every day. I often got it in the neck for nothing, when it was really Dad she was mad with.

When I finally did go to bed I had to creep round in the dark, and inevitably ended up falling on the bed in agony, picking bits of Lego out of my bare feet.

I think I could have handled that if Adam hadn't been

such a wrecker. He went through the room like Genghis Khan's Mongol horde. He ripped books and posters, ruined my Airfix models in an A-team car smash, spilt food and drink in bed – my bed, not his. Once, I found a sandwich festering in my shoe – a discovery I made with my foot!

Furthermore, he let Scraggy moult like an old dog all over my best black cords and sweater.

OK, so he missed playgroup and the garden and his friends – didn't we all? – but Mum should've kept him under control. It made me mad 'cos he got away with everything.

The only answer, short of wringing his neck, was to get out of the flat. I went off on my bike quite a bit. The trouble was it was winter, freezing cold and dark at five, so I couldn't stay out for very long. Mooching round the shops in town was warmer, but it just got frustrating 'cos I hadn't any spare cash, and I hadn't dared to borrow any more of Mum's twenty pences for weeks.

The crunch, when it came, was over my music tapes. Adam was irresistibly drawn to them – he just couldn't leave them alone. I came back from school one day to find my best 'Hits' tape festooned across the room in long brown streamers.

Grabbing him by the scruff of the neck, I hauled him downstairs and dragged him screaming through the flat in search of Mum.

'Just look what this little monster's done to my tape!' I yelled, shaking a fistful of mangled brown strings under her nose. Adam, still screaming, kicked me in the shins, so I shook him until his teeth rattled.

Mum leaned wearily over the sink. 'Put him down, Darrel, and stop causing trouble.'

I was outraged!

'Me?' I shouted, giving Adam another venomous shake.

'Me causing trouble? That's great! He wrecks my tape and I get the blame – as usual. That tape cost me six pounds – so who's going to buy me a new one? That's what I want to know.'

'*Shut up*, Darrel!' Mum braced her arms on the sink, stiff with tension. She looked ready to blow, but I was past caring.

'He gets away with everything. You and Dad never stop him. You're hopeless.'

'Darrel! Wait till your father . . . .'

'Oh yeah!' I sneered. 'Has he finally managed to fit us into his busy schedule?'

Everything got out of hand at that point, and all I can remember is Mum smacking me straight round the face with a wet hand. She put all her weight behind that smack, and it sounded just like a gun going off, knocking me right off my perch and bringing tears to my eyes.

I don't know what stopped me from hitting her back – but I'm glad now that I didn't – and two minutes later I was pedalling like a madman in the direction of Jackson's Bay.

Sitting on the rocks, my bike hidden in the scrub and brambles at the top of the cliff, I gradually pulled myself together.

Outwardly I must have looked the same as usual – apart from the inflamed hand-print on my face – but inwardly something had changed. The row with Mum had made all the anger and resentment knot up inside me until it was like a solid ball. As I sat there by the sea, chucking stones and shouting at Dad in my mind, that ball just got harder and bigger, until my face and chest ached with the effort of keeping it in.

Looking back, I know that was the turning-point. I'd had a choice – I could have gone to Dad, told him everything and tried to sort it out, but I'd decided that cold hostility would hurt him more.

It was freezing down by the water, but it was my favourite place when I was fed up – somewhere I could be alone and think things out. The wind blew the spray horizontally across the rocks, soaking my hair and clothes.

I stood up, hands thrust deep into the pockets of my anorak, and looked out over the wintery sea. A tanker, barely distinguishable in the half-light, was anchored out in the bay. Everything was grey, cold and gloomy.

Behind me I could see seagulls like scraps of white paper, tossing in the fierce up-draught from the cliffs. Hardly anybody knew the way down to this bay. Only me and my friend Stu – and his dad, of course. Most of our secret dens had been discovered by Stu's dad back in the fifties.

'Having this place to escape to is the only good thing in my life right now,' I thought despondently. 'This place to go to – and a friend like Stu.'

6

Making friends

I first met Stu after Dad smashed his hand in the trap-door not long after we arrived in Frinsham. He really hurt himself and couldn't use his hand for about ten days – then his thumbnail turned a horrible purplish-black and finally dropped off. Yucky, but fascinating!

The shop was open from eight-thirty in the morning till nine at night, six days a week – and part of Sunday, too. Crazy times – but it had always opened those hours, and Dad was determined to carry on the tradition.

Sometimes it got quite busy, so he took on Mrs Mitchell – Mrs M., we called her – to help for a couple of hours a day. Mum wasn't popular 'cos she hadn't volunteered for the job, but she had Grandma and Adam to think of – plus she wasn't in a mood to co-operate anyway.

Dad was in a real mess trying to move crates and things around with his injured hand, and they were much too heavy for me, but Mrs Mitchell's husband, Ted, turned up out of the blue one night with his son, Stuart, to help hump things up and down from the cellar. Ted suggested we form a human chain and we soon had all the stuff stashed away.

'Dad's a brickie,' said Stu conversationally as we shifted crates of pop from the shop to the cellar.

I hadn't the foggiest idea what he meant.

'A bricklayer,' he explained, seeing my puzzled expression. 'He can carry massive amounts of stuff up ladders – no trouble.'

I stopped, watching with interest as Mr Mitchell, nimble as a cat, carried heavy crates and boxes up and down the treacherous cellar steps. Stu was a smaller version of his dad – brown-haired and strongly built.

After that I saw quite a bit of Stu. He showed me places no-one else knew about – little meres out in the country, where we caught pink wormy things that sucked your blood. Ted said they did nothing of the sort, but we weren't convinced. Anyway, it was more interesting believing they did.

Stu also showed me ways down the cliffs into bays that looked inaccessible from above. But the best times – the ones I liked more than anything – were the fishing trips with his dad.

'It's the early birds that get the worms,' his dad would say, often turning up on our doorstep at quarter to seven in the morning, armed with two garden-forks and a bucket. Then the three of us would walk down to the sea, Ted striding ahead with a fork over his shoulder, whistling *Rule Britannia*, and me and Stu breaking into a trot to keep up.

Walking along the deserted beach, we'd search for worm-casts on the wet sand. Then, digging deep with our forks, we'd pick out the slimy wrigglers to use as bait for the night's fishing.

I could hardly wait till after tea to set off for the sea-front, armed with a cheese sandwich and a flask of coffee. At low tide we fished off the beach, close to the waves – but it was best when the tide was in, and we were on the slipway.

I was itching to do everything by myself 'cos I'd fished before, but Ted said sea-fishing was a bit different and insisted on casting the line for me the first few times.

'You've got to watch it with these sea rods,' he said, carefully turning the big wooden reel to bring the long row of hooks and lead sinkers up to the end of the rod. 'My dad made this one himself before the war. It's solid wood, and heavy! – not like your modern fibreglass ones.'

The sinkers must have been ten centimetres long, and the big metal hooks were armed with vicious barbs.

'I got hit by a lead sinker when I was a kid,' he said, balancing the rod in the crook of his arm and fixing worms firmly to the hooks. 'The doctors thought I was going to lose an eye – good job it wasn't a hook, or I would've done. Now, stand back.'

Holding the rod firmly in both hands, he swung the suspended row of hooks smoothly back – paused – then whipped the rod forwards with a powerful overarm stroke, releasing the reel and sending the weighted line hissing out to disappear into the darkness.

It was great leaning there on the railings, listening to the waves rising and falling against the sea wall, the lights of the town twinkling on the cliffs as we waited for the tug on the line that meant a catch. We hardly ever went home empty-handed from those trips – and nothing tastes better than a midnight feast of freshly-caught codling or whiting. Fantastic!

After saying that, it seems weird to say I hated Frinsham – but I did. I had great times with Stu, but as soon as I went back to the flat or was on my own, the good feelings just evaporated as though they'd never been, and I was eaten up with bitterness and resentment again.

Maybe I'd have felt differently if Stu had been at my school – at least I'd have had a friend around – but he went to the local comprehensive and I was over a mile away at Hurst Park – plus an extra half mile at night when I went the long way round to avoid the cemetery.

I reckon it was partly loneliness that got me involved with Simon Redfern's gang – plus the knowledge that Dad wouldn't like him. He used to be fussy about my friends, but now he was too busy even to notice that I didn't have any.

Simon was everything Dad warned me against, but he was friendly – and I needed a friend. Starting a new school is no picnic, but starting in the middle of a term when everybody's already paired off is really duff. I felt like a leper 'cos nobody talked to me much, and they made fun of my accent.

The spring term started off just the same – and then fate, in the shape of Simon Redfern, stepped in, and a note was pushed into my hand one afternoon during French:

Hey, new kid. What're you doing after school?

I'd seen a ripple of movement as the thin paper was passed from hand to hand along the row of kids, and I looked to see where it had come from, but all eyes were fixed innocently on the board where Mr Crane was writing up the French homework.

Turning the note over I wrote on the back:

Who wants to know?

The paper, which was thin and smelt faintly antiseptic, had a pale green monogram in the corner that I couldn't quite make out. I bent down to get a closer look, and nearly laughed out loud as I read the word 'Izal' – this stuff was school toilet-paper! After adding the words *Smart notepaper!* I sent the note back along the row, watching to see its final destination.

It landed on Si Redfern's desk and stopped. I knew Si – by reputation, anyway. He was a clever kid, but always in trouble over one thing or another.

The most persistent battle was over wearing mirror-shades during lessons. Mr Crane was one of the few teachers he didn't try it on with, so as he grinned back at me I could actually see his eyes, not just my own reflection.

He leaned over the desk and scribbled on a fresh sheet of paper. With his black hair, good looks and cheerful insolence, he was popular with the boys and madly fancied by most of the girls, and every new manoeuvre sent a thrill of anticipation through the class.

Super Si, at your service, the note read. *Don't complain about the paper – it's cheap, clean and available. Besides, write 'Izal' backwards and you've discovered what I aim to be in life. Get it?*

I looked again at the little green mark. What was he on about? L-A-Z-I? Ah – lazy! Well, he was pretty good at that already. I grinned at him and decided to give it a try:

Bike sheds – half three.

7

Simon says

So that was how our friendship started. We met in the sheds after school that day – me, Si, Jason, Keith and Lenny, and I fell straight into doing whatever Si said, just like all the others did.

'Right,' he announced, unlocking his bike, 'chips first, then down to the sea-front to play the videos.'

I did a quick calculation. I could manage the chips if I cut out a drink at lunch next day, but I'd have to give the video games a miss. (I wasn't really allowed to play on arcade machines anyway.)

A stab of discontent hit me. I'd always had plenty of spare cash in the past – pocket-money, paper-round, odd bits from Mum – but now I had barely enough to get the absolute essentials. I was going to feel a real wally if I had to keep saying 'no' to things Si wanted to do.

Outside the chip shop he got us all organised.

'Keith, watch the bikes. Lenny, get the chips. Give him your money, fellers.' He fished in his pocket and pulled out a handful of cash. 'Daz – here's sixty pence. Go next door and get us a bottle of cream soda.'

The sweet shop next to the chippy was run-down and not too clean. The old lady behind the counter had a cardigan the colour of sludge and a pair of prehistoric specs.

Si and Jason lounged casually in the background as I pushed the money across the counter and asked for the cream soda. The result was quite startling. She gave me a look that Medusa would have been proud of, then – seeing I didn't turn to stone – she ducked down behind the counter and began crashing about among the bottles of pop in what sounded like a serious effort to smash them all.

Re-emerging hot and flustered a couple of minutes later, she glared suspiciously at all of us before giving me the pop and the change.

'And another one bites the dust!' chortled Si as we rode away. Everybody except me laughed – I hadn't a clue what they were on about. But later, when we were sitting on a wall by the old aquarium, eating our chips and swigging cream soda from the bottle, it all became sickeningly obvious.

'I think that old bird has finally sussed us out,' sniggered Jason. 'We'll have to steer clear of her for a bit.'

'So what. I never liked that place anyway – it smells of mice.'

Si chucked his chip paper over the wall and wiped his hands on what looked like a floorcloth, but turned out to be a hanky – bind up a wound with that filthy rag and you faced certain death. 'I only went there 'cos she was thick,' he said.

'Is this a private conversation or can anyone join in?' I cut in testily, still completely in the dark.

Si looked at me appraisingly. 'Sure!' he said, fishing several slabs of chocolate out of his anorak pocket. 'Share the pickings – you earned it.'

I stared at the foil-wrapped bars, totally mystified. His eyebrows went up so far that they nearly met his hair.

'Don't tell me you didn't know we were pulling the old "faze and filch" routine!'

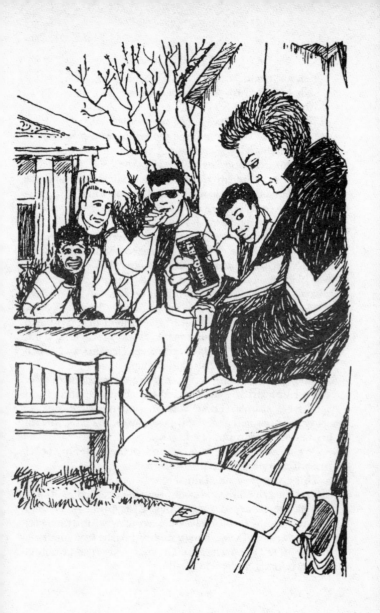

I shook my head.

'Never heard of "strike and snatch"?'

Another shake.

'Where have you been?' he boggled, chucking me a bar of chocolate. 'These are basic moves for land-pirates.' He bit off a chunk of Wholenut. 'Take that old biddy for instance – ripping her off is a doddle!'

Understanding hit me like a sledgehammer, and the chocolate suddenly looked about as inviting as a slug sandwich.

'But that's stealing!' I protested.

Si shrugged. 'So what? Everyone needs a hobby.'

He sat there on the wall, invisible behind his mirror sunglasses, sizing me up. If I left now they'd all think I was chicken, but if I stayed . . . . I looked down at the chocolate in my hands, trying to decide.

My first thought – What would Dad say? – was instantly followed by a knot of resentment that tightened in my stomach like a coiled snake. It was Dad's fault I was sitting here with no money, third-rate friends and stolen sweets. Who cared what Dad thought?

I looked up, staring coolly into Si's expressionless face. Then I unhurriedly unwrapped the chocolate and bit off a massive chunk. There was an imperceptible sigh as everyone breathed again and Jason broke the tension with his famous Fagin impersonation.

'We'll 'ave to show you the tricks of the trade, my boy!' he said, rubbing his hands together.

This time everyone laughed.

Grabbing the bikes, we rode along the deserted sea-front, past shuttered arcades and cafes. Everything was closed for the winter, and the place looked tatty with its peeling paint and piles of wind-blown rubbish. Apart from one cafe the only place open was Fun City, so we fastened our bikes to the railings and piled inside.

'The first thing to do in these places is a quick run round the payout slots,' said Si, meandering through the deafening noise of the arcade, sliding an exploratory hand into every machine.

'See,' he grinned triumphantly, holding out several coins collected from the 'Ten Penny Falls'. He tossed them into my hands. 'Here, you have it – I've got plenty.'

I felt a bit funny about being there at first 'cos I'd promised Mum I wouldn't play the machines – not after some kid at my other school got hooked on them and was in trouble with the police for stealing. But Si seemed to do OK. He put a lot of money in, and, as far as I could see, got plenty out.

'Easy peasy,' he bragged, 'You've just got to get into the system.'

Si said I lost 'cos I wasn't used to the machines, but all I could think of was what Mum would say if she found out I'd wasted half my dinner money in there. I didn't mean to spend it, but I couldn't give up when I was so near to winning, could I? Anyway, it was just bad luck.

I had another look round the slots hoping I could make it up, but no result, so I mooched off to watch Lenny on the Star Wars game.

'You're brilliant!' I said admiringly.

'That's 'cos I come here every night,' he commented, eyes alert, body tense, skilfully destroying the alien fighters. Zap! Whiz! 'And I always win free games.'

'How the heck does he get enough money to do this every night?' I wondered, watching him strafe the enemy with jagged bursts of his laser, his face bathed in eerie green light. In a lull between games I asked him where the money came from, but he tapped the side of his nose and said, 'Secret information.'

I was so busy watching him that I lost track of time, and what with going back the long way to avoid the cemetery,

I arrived home really late for tea. Mum was just draining some disgustingly overdone sprouts as I burst in through the door.

'We thought you were never coming,' she said with relief, transferring food from the oven to the table. 'Adam, tell Daddy that tea's ready. No – don't just shout! I could do that myself.'

I dumped my stuff and got out the squash and a jug of water.

'What's made you so late, Darrel?' she asked.

'I just went down the arcades with some other kids.'

'Arcades? You mean slot machines?' She stood still, holding the hot pie in oven-gloved hands. 'You know we don't like those places. You didn't spend any money, did you?'

I was faced with a major choice for the second time that day. I could either tell the truth and get a rocket, or I could lie.

'Nah – I just watched the others. Waste of money.'

She put the pie down and busied herself cutting it into wedges. 'I don't want you spending your time there, Darrel. If it's anything like the arcades in Newton Bridge it'll be full of all the rough kids. Promise me you won't go again.'

What could I do except agree? I lay in bed for hours that night, thinking over everything that had happened. My conscience was giving me a real hard time, but I didn't want to listen. After all, it wasn't me who pinched the chocolate in the first place – so why should I feel bad?

At the back of my mind I knew I should have given the stuff back to Simon and gone home, but it didn't seem that simple at the time.

And what was I going to do about my promise to Mum? – I'd already told Si that I'd go down the arcades again on Thursday.

What a mess!

I thought about chickening out, but couldn't face it, so in the end I decided to go just that once and tell him I wouldn't be going again.

Saintly Stu

The following Thursday I went to the arcade, but backed out of making it the last time. Before long it was a regular thing – three, sometimes four times a week.

Mum thought I was staying behind at school for football practice, and I was quite proud of how easily I could tell her barefaced lies. I got as good as Lenny on the machines, too, but finding the money for it was a bit of a problem.

For a while Si watched me carefully, never quite letting me in on things, and I took Keith's place as bike-guard and lookout while they did the business. But after a couple of weeks I was filed under 'OK' and taught the 'tricks of the trade'.

'S'easy,' said Simon, dipping a long spoon into his ice-cream soda in the warmth of the Harbour View cafe. 'It just needs some careful planning – picking the place, choosing the time and taking the chance.'

He licked his spoon, leaning forward conspiratorially to give me the details of his latest brainwave. After checking several times to make sure I'd understood, he ended with, 'After that – zap! Grab the stuff and scram.'

He relaxed, grinning. 'I call that little masterpiece "hit and run".'

'Works every time,' gloated Jason. 'But after a bit they

get wise so you have to give it a rest for a while. We'd been working the stunt with that old girl in the sweet shop for weeks before she cottoned on.'

There was a really nauseating drain-cleaner noise from Keith as he dragged the last drops of milkshake up his straw. Giving one final loud suck he pushed his empty glass to the middle of the table.

'The best one up to now was that off-licence near my house,' he grinned. 'You know – the feller that kept going to the cellar for bags of coal.'

They all guffawed.

'Yeah. We could've cleaned the place out.'

'What do you mean – could've. We did!'

And they all fell about laughing, telling me how they'd ripped off this bloke. But it gave me a nasty stab to think that it could've been my Dad – he had to go to the cellar for bags of coal. I'd never actually mentioned that we'd got a shop, and I didn't think they came over our side of town. But suppose they did?

'Hey, guys – do you think it's fair to pick on these small shops? They might be really struggling to make ends meet.'

'Come off it,' they mocked. 'Show us one of those shops without a Range Rover or a Volvo standing around outside – those folks are loaded.'

'Well, *my* dad hasn't got a Volvo,' I thought. 'Just a beat-up old van – and we're *always* short of money.' But I kept that information to myself and just vowed to make sure they didn't get near our shop.

Why didn't I run a mile when all this started? I don't really know. I think it was partly to get my own back on Dad. But also I was sick of not being able to have things I wanted. When I looked round, it seemed as though everybody had groovy clothes, money, trips out – everybody except me – and it wasn't fair.

All the kids at school – well, some of the kids – made

out that you were nobody if you didn't have 'style' – but 'style' cost money.

Si and Keith just said, 'So what!' But it was easy for them. Keith's dad was some big cheese at the hospital, and Si's was some sort of businessman, so they had stacks of pocket-money and could've easily bought most of the stuff we nicked. They only stole for kicks.

After that first time I just sort of accepted what they were doing. In fact, it gave me quite a thrill to sit there and listen to them, wondering how they got away with it – and even more of a thrill when I started joining in.

We were really psyched up when we hit a place, and I liked that feeling a lot. Soon I was as good as Simon at sizing up a situation and getting in and out fast. And it wasn't long before I graduated to stealing from the shops in town.

In Newton Bridge all the big shops had positively bristled with security systems and store detectives. By comparison, Frinsham was a shoplifter's paradise. The place had about as much security as a sieve, and we discovered all sorts of exciting ways of separating shopkeepers from their goodies.

My personal favourite involved carrying three garments into a changing-room, but only giving two back. It was tricky, but I got quite a few groovy bits that way – not too much, though, 'cos Mum started asking awkward questions, which I got round by saying they were swopped or borrowed from friends at school.

We solved the cash problem in all sorts of different ways. Lenny let me in on some of his dodges, so we worked as a team sometimes, going through another form's lockers together.

'Never mess up your own nest, you wally,' he hissed, dragging me out of our own third year lockers and into the second year's. 'We'd get massacred if we did our own form. If we don't hit them, they don't split on us.'

Most times we'd stand guard for each other and take turns to go through the pockets. But sometimes, if I got the chance, I'd ferret around on my own – although that was definitely trickier 'cos someone could walk in.

It beats me why kids leave money in the lockers – they're always getting warned about it. I'd never leave a thing in there.

In between times I was still knocking around with Stu – whose mum worked at our shop – and we had a lot of great times together, but every now and then something would happen and we'd fall out.

It was daft, really. Most of the stuff was only minor aggro, but he was so saintly that it got right up my nose. If shops undercharged us he'd tell them and give the money back. So if I didn't want to look like a villain I had to do the same. It was nauseating!

When I was with Si and the gang I never had bad feelings about keeping wrong change and that sort of thing. I mean, that was piffling stuff compared to the other things we did. But after a couple of hours with Stu my conscience felt like a tin of maggots.

Stu and I had one of our biggest bust-ups one evening cycling home from Jackson's Bay. I always insisted we went the long way round so that we didn't have to pass the cemetery in the dark. But that night he refused to do it, and we sat by the roundabout arguing the toss over which way to go.

'If we had to ride through the middle of it in the pitch dark, going the long way round would be common sense,' he said. 'But we don't have to do that. It's fifty metres of well-lit road, with a wall between us and the cemetery, and loads of folk about.

'I can even see your house from here, for Pete's sake! We end up having to cycle an extra half mile just to get

fifty metres from where we are now. I'm not going all that
way round just 'cos you're scared of ghosts – it's stupid!'

That got to me a bit 'cos I hadn't told him I was scared
of the dark and ghosts and things, he'd just sort of guessed
– maybe 'cos I'd once told him about Kev's books. In
fact, that had been one of our first arguments – he'd said
they were mind-bending rubbish and I'd said they were
fantastic.

Most times Stu's OK, but when something like that
comes up he starts bringing God into it – as if God would
be bothered about what you read! I'd felt quite
embarrassed for him. But then all this business over the
cemetery brought it up again.

'I wouldn't want to spend a lot of time in there,' he said.
'It's a miserable place. And you never know what sort of
weirdos are wandering around. But I'll be blowed if I'm
going to stop riding past. Anyway, why do you read that
creepy rubbish when it makes you so scared?'

I could feel the maggots shifting uneasily in my stomach
again, just like they always did when Stu started taking
the lid off the can. I don't know how he always got it right,
but he did, and I could've throttled him.

'It's got nothing to do with what I read,' I objected hotly.
But it had.

I'd just pinched a couple of real spine-chillers and was
reading them under the covers at night. OK, so I'd been
having a bit of trouble getting to sleep afterwards. But I
liked those sort of books and I wasn't going to give them up.

'It's got everything to do with it,' he argued, 'Your
mind's so full of that tripe that it's affecting what you do.
You read the stuff, and you're petrified about what might
grab you in the dark. God's right when he says to keep
junk out of your mind . . . .'

'Here we go,' I interrupted nastily. 'Sounds like God
sits on your shoulder like a parrot. Squa-a-a-wk! Who's

a pretty boy, then?'

Maybe I shouldn't have done that; his religion meant a lot to him. But I had to shut him up 'cos it always spooked me to hear him talking as though God was actually around. If you ask me, people who believe that stuff are hooked on the biggest ghost story of all time.

Anyway, he wouldn't give in – just cycled stubbornly off towards the shop, forcing me to put my head down and belt after him at top speed.

Stuart Super-saint Holy Joe Mitchell. I could have bashed him in for making me do that.

9

Beach battle

' "Doctor, doctor," ' quoted Si, as we lounged around one afternoon behind the pavilion in the museum gardens, ' "I'm always stealing things." '

He struggled to keep his face straight as the rest of us waited for the punch-line.

' "Here, take these pills, and if you're no better in a fortnight, get us a colour telly." '

I'd meant to laugh, but instead it came out as a strangled honk 'cos my drink went down the wrong way and I thought I was going to choke. Coke sprayed out of my nose and mouth and I rolled around on the bench fighting for breath.

'You filthy beggar, Chadwick!' they yelled, leaping backwards to avoid contamination. I brushed myself down and looked over at Stu. He was laughing – but I could tell he wasn't really happy.

This was the first time he'd come with me to meet Si and the others, and it hadn't exactly been a howling success. It wasn't his fault, I suppose. He'd tried hard to be friendly, but they just weren't his sort.

The trouble was, I kept seeing them through his eyes. All their off-colour jokes and talk stuck out like a sore thumb. And the swearing! Normally I didn't hear it, but that day every word was like a hot needle being jabbed into me.

What was bothering me was if one of them let anything slip about the shop-lifting. I wished I'd never brought him along.

We split up later. Si and the others nipped off to the arcades, but Holy Joe said it wasn't his scene, and I could hardly just abandon him could I? So we went the other way and cycled out along the old brick pipe that went past the headland and out into the sea.

The landward side of the pipe was great for kids. It was protected from the worst of the storms and tides and had a beach and a shallow sandy pool full of starfish, small crabs and seaweeds that looked like green and red lettuce. The other side was to the open sea, with thick ropes of sea-belt and oarweed, and slippery mats of brown wrack hiding the rocks.

The tide was coming in, and the trick was to wait until it was level with the top of the pipe and then race back to the steps with water arching out from under the tyres. If you did it fast enough the water sprayed up level with your shoulders. Good fun usually – but not today.

It was murder sitting there waiting for the tide to come in. Stu was just messing around with his brakes and not looking at me, and I was having all sorts of conversations in my mind of the 'He'll say, then I'll say' variety.

After a few minutes of that I was all psyched up and ready to blow like a pressure-cooker, and the words, when they came, burst out packed with accusation.

'Well, Your Holiness, I take it you don't think much of my friends.'

Why I hit him with it like that I don't know – except that at that moment I didn't think much of them, either, and it'd given me a bad dose of guilt. Somebody – probably Stu as usual – had poked around and got the maggots on the move again.

'They're all right,' he muttered non-committally, still fiddling about with his bike.

'Come off it!' I scoffed, 'You thought they were rubbish – I could see it written all over your face.'

He looked up, disconcerted by the fierceness of my attack, wondering how to answer me. Would he have the guts to say what he really thought? Part of me wished he would, even though I'd hate him for it.

He leaned his forearms on the handlebars of his bike. 'You think they're OK, then?'

'Yeah, course I do. Why shouldn't I?'

He shrugged. 'Just wondered why you were so edgy.'

'Me? Edgy? I'm not edgy.'

'Come off it, Daz. Every time one of those guys opened his mouth you were sweating blood. Anyone would think they'd got something on you.'

My stomach lurched and I tried to get a grip on things. Was he joking, or wasn't he? I could feel the sweat breaking out all over me again. Any minute now he was going to say, 'And how long have you been a thief?' Then I'd go to pieces and tell him everything.

I stared into his steady blue eyes feeling as though I'd got *shop-lifter* stamped on my forehead in fluorescent letters. Luckily he went back to fiddling with the brakes before the sweaty redness reached my face, so he never noticed.

I turned into the wind in an effort to cool my blazing cheeks.

'I can't put my finger on it,' he said after a minute, 'but I just don't feel good about those guys. I get the impression that hanging about with them could mean real trouble.'

'Just 'cos they swear doesn't mean . . . .'

'It's got nothing to do with swearing.' He pushed his hood back and stared out over the sea. 'Ninety per cent of our friends swear like troopers, but that doesn't make them villains, does it? It's something else.'

He paused, searching for words. 'All those jokes about stealing – like the one about his Mum pinching dresses so that she'd have something smart to wear in court – stuff like that. It sounds funny, but,' he shrugged, 'I get a lot of bad feelings from that kid Simon. The rest of them just follow him like sheep.'

He hesitated, looking into my face, testing my reactions.

'There's something else I'm not happy about. I can't tell you exactly what's changed, but you're not the same now as you were even a few weeks ago. You probably don't notice, but you've started coming out with all sorts of weird ideas and duff attitudes – and now I know where these ideas are coming from. Honest, Daz, those lads are trouble with a big T.'

OK, so he was right. But I still wanted to smash his face in – the pompous, religious prig! Maybe Si and the gang were bad news, but he'd got a nerve saying so, even though I'd asked him for his opinion.

Saintly Stu! So what, if he didn't rate them. I liked hanging around with them and doing what we did.

Water was creeping round the sole of my trainer now, and I stood poised with one foot on the crumbling brickwork and the other on the pedal, watching it lap against my front tyre.

Times like this I felt like I was two different people. The old Daz was sick of lies and deceit – and the new one just wanted to make up his own rules and live for kicks without any interference. My mind was a battleground – just a jumbled mass of conflicting thoughts and feelings, dominated more and more by what Simon said.

Stu Mitchell was just a killjoy. It was stupid to get worked up over his scabby opinion. Resentment flooded my mind as the first rush of cold sea-water crept over my shoes.

'You know nothing, Mitchell,' I spat nastily. 'They're

better than your boring youth group fairies any day –
prancing about and praying and making stupid canoes!'
(I'd actually been quite jealous about the canoes, but catch
me telling him that – even canoes wouldn't get me
running with that crowd.)

That got to him. It narked him when I called him 'Your
Holiness' and things like that, but then he'd just shrug it
off and laugh. But say something about his pals. Wow!
He defended his pals to the hilt.

'Well at least I can tell my mum the truth about who
I'm with and what I'm doing,' he retorted, stung by my
attack. 'I don't have to lie and say I'm at football when
I'm really down the arcades with those jokers. You're a
liar, Chadwick!'

Now how the heck did he know that?

I flicked back through the afternoon's conversations.
Blasted Jason! Trust him to let it out that we went there
nearly every day.

'And don't think I've only just found out. I've known
for ages that you weren't staying behind for football.'

'Who said?'

'Never mind who said – it's the truth, isn't it? It's
bothered me for ages about you lying to your folks, but
I was too scared to say anything to you. But now . . . .'

The sea had completely soaked my trainers as it poured
smoothly over the pipe, streaming down its slippery green
sides and filling the shallow pool on the landward side.

'I'm going!' I said angrily, forcing past him and shoving
Stu's bike out of the way with my hand.

Normally there was just room to pass if you were careful.
But this time I wasn't careful, and my sudden move sent
him lurching too near the sloping sides of the pipe. His
trainers slipped on the slimy bricks and he and his bike
slithered gracelessly down the green slope to land among
the rocks and seaweed a metre below.

His face was a picture – and so were his clothes, wet to the waist and covered in green slime.

As I'd watched him lose his balance and crash down the slope my heart had leapt into my mouth. Spread-eagled across the rocks, frozen with shock, there was no telling what damage might have been done. His bike could have been smashed up – and so could he I suppose, although that seemed less serious at the time.

But both looked OK – just seaweedy and wet. Anger melted into remorse as I watched him struggle to his feet. Reaching down, I helped him drag his bike back on to the pipe.

'Sorry, pal.'

'No sweat.'

That's one great thing about Stu – he never holds grudges.

I crouched down, water from the rising tide narrowly missing the seat of my jeans as I checked Stu's machine for anything drastic.

'No sweat,' he said again, bending to pick limp, green, lettuce-like weed out of the spokes.

'For Pete's sake let's get home so I can wring out my boxer-shorts!'

10

Shop-lift mode

After that, things went right down the tubes.

For a start, I got caught at school with another kid's dinner tickets, and all sorts of trouble erupted as a result. Dad went bananas, while Mum was weepy and reproachful.

I swore blind I was the victim of a terrible mistake. Luckily I got away with it, but it really put the wind up me – especially when I discovered that Si had tried to pinch something from our shop that week.

Dad caught him in the act and, thinking he was a first offender, let him off with a warning. Wow, if he only knew!

When Dad gave his description to Mum and Mrs M. I knew it must have been Si. Good job I wasn't in the shop when he turned up. Dad would've murdered me if he thought I hung around with kids like him.

It was best to keep a low profile for a bit, so I cooled it at school and left Dad's cash untouched on the bedroom mantelpiece – not that he'd ever noticed the odd fifty pence piece go missing, but he just might start to put two and two together after the dinner ticket business.

Si would be a fool to go in our shop again. But what if he did? What if he saw me there and Dad found out we hung around together?

Fear of being found out made me think seriously about giving up stealing altogether. I was sure I could if I wanted to. There were lots of nights when I lay staring into the dark, determined that I was never, ever going to pinch anything again – and I meant it.

But as soon as my mind drifted towards sleep it slipped automatically into shop-lift mode – running through an unending mental maze of hits, dodges and narrow escapes, until I was convinced that I was irreversibly programmed to steal. That's a pretty frightening idea, I can tell you.

Everywhere I went my mind automatically worked out the potential gains and risks – Grandma's purse, Dad's till, supermarket shelves, unguarded pockets and handbags – you name it, I worked out a way to pinch from it. Stealing became my way of life, and I was taking risks even Si thought were long shots.

'You're nuts, Chadwick!' he'd say, his eyebrows crawling into his hair as I outlined a particularly risky job, 'That's a suicide run. Are you tired of living or something?'

It's easy to say that I should have steered clear of Si and the others – you couldn't be with them without getting roped in – but I didn't have any other pals, did I? Except Stu, of course.

Things were pretty awful with him and me. His mum kept asking me round to the house when she saw me at the shop, but I just handed her some line about being busy. I don't think she believed me for a minute, and – knowing His Holiness – he'd have told her everything anyway. The rat!

He still came to call for me sometimes, and we'd head off for our secret den in the old wartime artillery target bunkers at Jackson's Bay. But it's hard to have fun in a secret den when you're not really talking to the bloke you're with.

Once, thinking it'd be easier if we were in a crowd, I

asked him if he fancied going off round Barton Mere with me and the gang.

'Thanks, but count me out,' he said, manhandling his bike across the stepping-stones linking the cliffs with the prom.

'I asked my dad about Si and the others – not mentioning names or anything,' he added hastily, seeing my face flush.

'I told him how I felt – about them being shady and all that. I thought he'd say I was being daft, but he didn't. He said God often gave him warnings like that, and it was best to take them seriously. Don't worry. He doesn't know it's anything to do with you.'

Well, God was right this time, except that he hadn't warned Stu to steer clear of me. But if he hadn't shopped me to his dad, maybe he hadn't blabbed to his mum either. I decided to check.

'Have you told anybody else?'

'No – but Mum's wondering why we don't go off together as much as we did.'

We cycled along the sandy prom and up past the first-aid hut.

'I told her you were busy,' he said unhappily. 'I can't say I feel good about it though. I've always talked to Mum and Dad about everything, but I didn't want to land you in trouble, what with Mum working in your dad's shop.'

Like I said, he defended his pals to the hilt.

The following Saturday morning, me and Stu nipped into town for a look round the shops, breaking off at about half eleven to have a snack in a cafe. We ordered Coke and hot doughnuts, and fought our way back through the crowd to the only empty booth in the place.

'Back in a minute,' said Stu, disappearing in the direction of the toilets.

Sitting with my back to the street, I didn't see Si push

open the doors and make his way towards me, with Jason, Keith and Lenny trailing in his wake.

'Well, look who's here, fellers!' he crowed, clapping me heavily on the back just as I bit into the doughnut. 'It's Mr Darrel Con-artist Chadwick – scourge of the superstore.'

The combination of the thump, the shock and the doughnut going down the wrong way was devastating, and we had action-replay of the scene in the museum gardens – only this time it definitely wasn't funny.

'Shut your face, Redfern!' I wheezed, fighting for breath. 'Any remarks like that in front of Stu and I'll fill you in.'

'Well, pardon me for living,' he said, pretending to look shocked.

The four of them pushed into the seats round me and Si took a bite of my abandoned doughnut. 'What's a serious con-man like you doing with an idiot like him anyway?' he said with his mouth full.

'He's not an idiot!' I snapped, stung by Si's contemptuous tone. 'He's a good laugh. Better than you lot any day. You'd better keep your mouth shut – he's coming back.'

The place was packed – it always is on a Saturday – and Stu had to force his way back from the loo between queues of people stacked fifteen deep. His smile faded abruptly when he found his seat occupied by Si, and he stood, hands in pockets, looking totally cheesed off.

Si lounged indolently in the booth, his arms stretched across the backrest.

'Hi, Stu,' he simpered from behind his blank, silvery mirror shades, in a syrupy tone that set my teeth on edge.

I looked apprehensively at Stu.

'Hi.'

Stu's reply was about as inoffensive as it could be, but

it did nothing towards neutralising the ill-will that crackled
through the air like electricity.

'For Pete's sake, you guys,' griped Lenny nervously,
'are we going to sit here all day?'

'Yeah,' I cut in hastily to break the Gunfight at the OK
Corral confrontation. 'Let's make a move. Me and Stu
are off to Taplow's 'cos I need a new pen. Why don't you
come along?'

'Why not?' said Si, turning away abruptly. 'Let's go.'

The gang stood up and made for the door, leaving me
and Stu getting our stuff together to follow them.

'Hey, Daz.' Stu grabbed my arm. 'What did you say
that for? Can't we just go off by ourselves?'

'Have a heart, Stu. You two were giving each other the
"drop dead" treatment. What else could I do? I just said
the first thing that came into my head. They'll get fed up
after ten minutes and push off somewhere else, you'll see.'

He wasn't happy, but I couldn't afford to get Si's back
up. Anyway, we'd only be together for ten minutes. I
mean, what could possibly go wrong in ten minutes?

The pavements were packed with shoppers, so we were
nearly at Prince Street before we found the others. I was
even beginning to think my troubles were over, that we'd
lost them completely – but then I saw Lenny waving from
Sullivan's doorway.

'Simon says we'll just have a look round in here first
'cos they've just got a load of new stuff in for the summer.'

I looked at Stu. 'It's only for a minute . . . .'

We pushed open the door and followed Lenny in.

11

Nightmare at Sully's Store

Sullivan's Store was typical of its kind – cheap souvenirs, posters, crummy tee-shirts, and bits of collectable stationery such as fancy rubbers and things.

Lots of the stuff's pretty off-colour in one way or another – some of it downright vulgar – so I knew Stu wouldn't be overjoyed if we stuck around for long. I think some of it's funny, but he says, 'Would I fancy showing it to my mum?'

The answer is, *'No way!'*, so maybe he's got a point.

Si had a nerve going there. The gaffer had very nearly caught him pinching some stuff only a couple of weeks before, and his eyes had been glued to us ever since we'd walked in.

Squinting through a gap in the display I could see him watching Si and Lenny from behind his cash register and signalling to his assistant to keep an eye on the rest of us.

Big hope! For a start she was as blind as a bat, but more important, she always ended up watching the wrong folks, so we usually just ignored her and got on with the job.

Stu was in a corner trying on sunglasses, so I ambled over to join him.

'Get a load of these,' he said, appearing from behind

the stand in a pair that sparkled like Niagara Falls in sunlight.

'They're gross!' I protested. 'You look like Dame Edna.'

'Yeah – and you should see the price,' he said with awe, replacing them carefully on the stand.

I hardly heard him. I'd just spotted the desire of my heart. Something I'd wanted for months – a pair of shades like Si's, only better by light-years. They were the grooviest pair of shades I'd ever seen, and I decided there and then that they belonged to me.

They must have cost well over ten quid, but I didn't bother checking the price 'cos I never paid anyway.

I glanced round furtively. No-one was watching me. Stu had wandered off towards the stationery, and everybody else was playing hide-and-seek among the mugs and novelties. So with as little movement as possible I removed the shades from their place on the rack and slipped them into my pocket.

Next minute, Si and the others, tired of baiting the shop staff, came over to join me, jostling each other in their efforts to get to the sunglasses.

They were just going through the Dame Edna routine again when Stu appeared at my elbow and said in a low voice, 'C'mon, Daz. They're going to be ages. Let's say we're bombing off somewhere else. I've got to be home by two, and it's half past twelve now.'

'What's up, Pea-brain?' said Si, eyeing him through a pair of Dennis Taylor Snooker Specs. 'Don't you like our company?'

'Not a lot,' said Stu stiffly.

'Come on, guys, keep it cool,' I pleaded. 'Let's go.'

Si shrugged and turned away.

'The stuff here's trash anyway,' he said loudly for Sully's benefit. Then, hefting his bag on to his shoulder, he headed past the till to the door.

'One moment, sonny.' Mr Sullivan's arm shot across the doorway, blocking Si's exit. 'I have reason to believe that one or more of your party may have items on their person that are not paid for. Therefore I must ask you to empty your bags and pockets.'

With his pompous tone, purple nose and bristling moustache he was ludicrous – like a character from a bad film.

But I wasn't laughing. I stood rooted to the spot, cold waves of panic sweeping over me, the frames of the stolen shades digging into my hip-bone through the thin lining of my jacket. Already in my mind I could see the police, the publicity – Mum and Dad.

I had to think – but I couldn't! My face drained of colour and I felt horribly sick, but no-one noticed 'cos all eyes were on the action in the doorway where Si and Lenny were giving Sully a load of cheek. Their cocky behaviour could only mean they were clean – which in itself was some sort of miracle. I watched in silent panic as, one by one, they emptied the junk out of their pockets and on top of the counter.

Oh, no. Oh, no. What am I going to do?

Getting out of the shop was impossible 'cos Sully had shut the door. I couldn't drop the shades on the floor or put them back 'cos someone would notice.

So I did the only other thing I could think of. I dropped them gently into Stu's carrier without his knowing and slid quietly sideways to position myself innocently on the other side of the group.

It would have been a lousy thing to do to my worst enemy – but I'd done it to my best friend!

That's what happens when you press the panic button – you do the first crazy thing that comes to mind. Self-preservation is definitely the name of the game.

'Now you,' said Sully, pointing to me as Keith scooped

up the filthy contents of his pockets. 'Let's see what you've got.'

The others were still doing a noisy 'injured innocence' routine as I spread my stuff out on the counter. There wasn't much – a couple of Biros (one leaking), a stump of pencil, a couple of quid in change, dinner tickets, fruit-gums – certainly no stolen property.

Sully was starting to look slightly doubtful.

'Well,' I scoffed, smirking at Si and the others, 'that was a waste of everybody's time.'

Sweeping my stuff off the counter, I redistributed it through my pockets and swaggered insolently to the door. Stu followed looking dead unhappy.

'Just a minute, sonny,' barked Mr Sullivan, grabbing Stu's sleeve as he was about to leave the shop. 'Let's see if we strike gold with you.'

Oh, *no!* The realisation hit me like a sledgehammer: he's actually going to search Stu!

I never thought he'd do that. I mean, Stu wasn't even part of the gang.

I'd figured that Sully would know that – but why should he? I hadn't reckoned that just by being with us Stu had become a suspect. He'd been tarred with the same brush, even though he was innocent.

The next half-hour was a nightmare. I stood by and watched while Stu, embarrassed but confident, emptied first his pockets then his bag. I saw his expression change to shocked disbelief as the stolen shades clattered lightly on to the counter bearing their triangular silver tag with the sticky, orange 'Sullivan's Store' label.

I heard him protest his innocence, even looking to me for support – 'Daz, you know me. Tell him I wouldn't do it!' – but I just shrugged and shook my head.

'Well, who'd have thought it?' whispered Lenny as Sully sent his assistant off to ring the police. 'Just shows you.

I'd have said he was the last person to go in for that sort
of thing.'

'Yeah,' gloated Jason, 'and he reckons he's a Christian.'

'Cut it out!' I hissed, jabbing Jason viciously with my
elbow and hearing a satisfactory 'Oof!' of pain.

I wanted to run – but I couldn't. I knew I had to stay
and see it to the end, even though I'd do nothing to help
him.

Out of the corner of my eye I could see Si – shades in
hand – watching me, his black eyes narrow and
appraising.

After a minute the others moved away and he sidled
over.

'You planted those shades on him, didn't you?' he
whispered, his breath tickling my ear.

'Get lost!' I hissed, trying to sound outraged.

'Betcha did,' he insisted.

'What would I do that for? He's my pal.'

'You don't fool me for a minute, Chadwick. I saw you
sweating when Sully stopped us.' He laughed. 'With
friends like you, who needs enemies?'

'Bog off!'

Stu was still claiming he was innocent when the police
arrived. He must have known someone had set him up –
so why didn't he say anything? Why didn't he point the
finger at us?

They did ask us a few questions, but there was no reason
for them to suppose Stu hadn't pinched the shades. I mean,
everybody claims they're innocent at first, don't they? So
after a bit they let the rest of us go.

I didn't go far – just to a shop doorway further up the
street, where I watched as an interested crowd gathered
to see the police take Stu from the shop to the waiting squad
car. They passed me as they drove off up the main street,
and I caught a glimpse of Stu's white face as the car nosed

into the busy Saturday traffic and was gone.

I ran, non-stop, through the town-centre crowds, down Northcliffe Road, along past the pool and the beach bungalows, leaping dangerously across the slimy stepping-stones to the sandy cliffs at the other side.

Racing to the top I threw myself down the steep, brambly path that led to our secret den in the old target shelters. Thorny stems caught at my coat and trousers as, sobbing with shame and exertion, I flung myself down the remains of the rusty ladder.

Then, utterly drained, I slid my back down the pitted concrete wall and crouched there, letting black waves of fear and self-loathing engulf me.

12

Massive frame-up

I didn't go home till about five-thirty – just spent all afternoon in the den telling myself I'd done the only sensible thing and fighting the urge to confess.

Stu'd be OK. They didn't prosecute kids like him – first offenders and all that. At least, I didn't think they did. Besides, folks from his church would say what a good lad he was.

I sneaked in the house as quietly as I could, but Mum pounced on me like a starving lion as soon as the door opened, so I knew she'd already heard the news.

'Where *have* you been all afternoon?' she demanded. 'And what's been going on, for heaven's sake? Your dad's going mad, and we can't get a word of sense out of anybody.'

Not waiting for an answer, she opened the shop door and yelled, 'Brian, can you come?'

Dad's reply was incomprehensible to me, but she shut the door and turned back with both barrels loaded, ready to start firing questions.

I could handle being cross-examined by Dad – he's easily side-tracked – but I didn't want to be left alone with Mum. She's got all the dedication and skill of the Spanish Inquisition when it comes to interrogation, and it was only

the traffic-stopping condition of my clothes that saved me
from the mental equivalent of having my toe-nails torn off.

'What have you done to your best coat?' she demanded,
grabbing me by the collar and thwacking clouds of dirt off
my back with her other hand. 'And your trousers! They're
all torn and filthy. My word, Darrel,' she hooted, as Dad
came in from the shop, 'you've got some explaining to do!'

Dad pulled a chair out from under the table and sat
down, saying, 'I've locked up for a bit so we can get to
the bottom of this.'

'Wow!' I thought. 'Wonders'll never cease.' Dad had
never shut the shop before for anything.

'Darrel, what's all this about Stuart getting caught shop-
lifting? Mum and I just can't believe it – not Stuart.'

'Mrs M. was devastated when the police rang,' said
Mum, still bashing away at my back, 'so Dad went with
her to the police-station while I looked after the shop.'

Dad ran a troubled hand through his hair. 'Ted was out
all afternoon so he's only just heard. It'll have hit him hard
– he thinks the world of that boy.'

'We want to know what happened,' said Mum, dragging
my coat off and attacking it with a clothes-brush. 'Stuart
mentioned some boys from your school and a kerfuffle in
a shop, but we can't make sense of it 'cos he was really
too upset to talk.'

She put the coat down and waved the brush angrily
under my nose. 'We've been waiting for you all afternoon
– where've you been?'

Adam burst in at that point demanding food, so
Grandma – who'd been sitting quietly listening – hustled
him out into the kitchen. Glad of the interruption, I groped
frantically for a way out. What could I say? More to the
point, how much did they already know?

It would help if I knew what Stu had said. Had he spilt
the beans about Si and the arcades and all that? Maybe

not, 'cos Mum would already be going bonkers about it
if he had. Best to stick as near to the truth as I could.

'I dunno what happened, Dad,' I mumbled, carefully
detwigging my trousers to avoid looking at him. 'We met
some kids from school in a cafe and ended up looking round
Sully's with them. The guy who owns the place picked on
these other kids and searched them – but they were clean.
And then . . . .'

I glanced up to see how he was taking it.

'. . . then he found the shades in Stu's bag and called
the police.'

I went back to picking bits off my pants. 'I was pretty
upset, so I went off up the cliffs by myself.'

They went over and over it, asking loads of questions.
Was I sure the glasses hadn't just dropped into Stu's bag?
Had he meant to pay and just forgotten? Who were these
other kids? Why had Mr Sullivan picked on them? Could
one of them have planted the sunglasses on Stuart?

Sticking to the same story all the time wasn't easy, and
I could feel a guilty flush rising up my neck as the questions
got nearer the mark. I had to hide my face somehow, so
I got up and went to the sink for a glass of water, keeping
my back turned until the colour in my cheeks subsided.

It was a horrible few minutes. I had to steer the talk away
from Si and the gang – I couldn't let Dad even think of
contacting them!

But that left Stu without an atom of defence. I felt terrible
about it until I realised that we'd just spent three-quarters
of an hour discussing the fate of Mr Wonderful – but Dad
never had time to spend even five minutes talking to me.
Catch him closing the shop 'cos I was in trouble!

Resentment boiled over in a corrosive torrent and I
slammed my glass down on the draining-board.

'He was caught redhanded, wasn't he?' I flared. 'Why
shouldn't he have pinched them? How come everybody

thinks he's so blinking perfect?'

Mum and Dad just gaped at me as I barged past them, flinging the door open so violently that it smashed a chunk out of the cupboard. Dad leapt up and followed me, but I locked myself in the loo and wouldn't talk to him.

I could hear him reassuring Grandma that I was 'just a bit upset about young Stuart' – absolute proof that he knew nothing about anything.

After that, I avoided everybody like the plague. It wasn't easy, and I knew Si well enough to realise he'd want to cash in on his suspicions.

He did make life hell – always hinting, always dropping remarks to show he hadn't forgotten. But he couldn't say too much 'cos I knew enough about him and his pals to nail them to the wall – though he made every shot count.

'Has Holy Joe pinched any more sun-specs lately?' he'd ask innocently, giving Keith and Lenny a withering look as they guffawed behind him.

'Don't mock,' he scolded sanctimoniously. 'Stu needed those shades to cut down the glare from his halo. Not that it'll be glaring a lot right now!'

They fell about laughing, but Si whispered, 'If he needs new frames he can come to you, can't he? After all, you framed him last time.'

He lowered his mirror shades and leered at me.

'But what's a frame-up between friends?'

It all got a bit much, particularly in class.

'Hey, Daz,' he'd jibe, grinning through a hole in a piece of Izal paper, 'I've been framed!'

The only answer was to keep well away from all of them, so I took to skipping school (it was near the end of term anyway) and hid, Rambo-like, in the old target bunker. Concealed by the undergrowth, I saw a potential enemy in every innocent dog-owner or coastal-path walker.

I worried at first that Stu might turn up. But he soon

got the message that I didn't want to see him – a few deliberate snubs and a bit of obvious evasion did the trick.

If things had been different it would have been a fantastic summer, but I had no-one to share it with. Lonely days were followed by lonely evenings, and because it stayed light until quite late it was often nearly ten o'clock before I rolled up at home.

Mum got upset about it because she and Dad had made an effort to get time off for us to do things together again – even taking on extra help in the shop so that he could get away. But I knew they were just angling for me and Dad to have man-to-man chats, and I wasn't falling for that.

I'd succeeded in cutting myself off from everybody. There was just one massive snag. Cutting people off outside was easy, but what about all the junk inside? Why didn't it all go when I got rid of Stu and Si and Dad?

Everywhere I went words would leap out at me from TV reports, newspapers and conversations, until I was sure that *thief* and *shoplifter* were written over my head in flashing lights.

Even the advertising hoarding that I cycled past every day – *J. Dawson – Decorators, Joiners and Shopfitters* – leapt out at me as *Joiners and Shop-lifters*. It might sound funny, but it really got me down.

By comparison, stopping stealing wasn't hard. I suppose it helped not seeing the gang or going to the arcades any more. But I still thought about it all the time, and I couldn't escape the memories and the guilt.

All the stuff I'd stolen kept going through my mind, adding up like a massive bill at the supermarket – one thing after another. And all the time I was panicking 'cos I knew I'd have to pay for it in the end. I tried making excuses but there was no escape. I was a thief, dozens of times over – and I'd betrayed my best friend to save my own skin.

Stu's name cropped up everywhere. Mum would ask Mrs M. about him, or I'd overhear kids talking in the street. I couldn't get away from it.

I suppose things hadn't gone too bad for him legally. He'd been cautioned by the police, but as it was his first offence it hadn't gone any further, just like I'd predicted. Dad said it didn't matter if the case was dropped or not; Stu had a record now and it would always go against him.

Another really horrible thing was that everybody got to know about it, and some folks really took him apart – especially 'cos he was a Christian. I suppose it gave them a chance to feel a bit smug. Anyway, his reputation was completely blown, and they made sure he knew it.

Stu's dad, Ted, came to see me the day after Stu's arrest, but I just stuck to the story I'd told Dad. He watched my face all the time I was speaking – a lousy trick which knocked me off my stroke a bit. But he seemed to believe me.

The worst moment was right at the end, just when I thought I was safe.

'Well, never mind, son,' he said quietly, sitting back in the armchair. 'You and me know Stuart would never have stolen those glasses – and God knows, too. We'll just leave him to sort it out, shall we?'

After that I tried to blot the whole thing out of my mind. But thoughts kept turning up uninvited, and I found myself actually groaning out loud with guilt.

I was sure things couldn't possibly get worse – but I was wrong.

13

Cliff-top drama

'This is the last straw, Darrel,' said Mum in a poisonous
tone, as she plunged her hand down the loo and tugged
at the sodden mass wedged firmly in the bend of the pipe.
'This is positively the last straw.'

'You always say it's my fault,' I objected, giving Adam
a baleful glare as he clung, bawling, to Grandma, doing
his dying duck act. 'You try sharing a room with the
little . . . .'

'*Darrel!*'

'I don't care. He's a little *scab!*'

Grandma, who didn't usually take sides, gave me a
deeply reproachful look. 'But, Scrags,' she said, rocking
Adam in her arms, 'you know how he feels about Scrags.'

'Well, what about my planes?' I thought viciously. No-
one gave a hoot about the hours I'd spent collecting those
pictures and sticking them on my bit of the attic wall –
only for that little blister to destroy the lot in five minutes.

He's lucky it was Scrags I flushed down the toilet and
not *him*.

Mum withdrew her arm from the loo and sat back on
her heels with an angry snort. Scrags was still down there
and water was lapping dangerously close to the rim.

'I can't move the blasted thing,' she snapped, 'We'll

have to wait till Dad comes.'

This information brought new howls from Adam, but Mum gave him a swipe and told him to put a sock in it.

'Nobody – and I mean nobody – touches this toilet until Dad's got that blanket out of there,' she ordered, just keeping the lid on her temper.

'If you need to go, you'll have to ask Mavis next door if you can use hers. I'm sorry, Mother, but that's all we can do.' And with a glare in my direction she stomped downstairs.

Bitterly angry, I shut myself in the attic and tried piecing together what remained of my pictures – but it was no use, they were totally ruined. I couldn't save any of them. Screwing the lot into a ball, I hurled them across the room and flung myself on the bed, letting waves of anger roll over me.

I lay there, my mind exploding with malice towards Mum and Adam, letting the fierce current of anger carry me into its malignant whirlpool. Everyone was against me. My mind spawned lurid scenes of vengeance, and I imagined Adam, Dad, Si, Stu – all my enemies – sprawled at my feet full of cringing remorse.

But once caught in the whirlpool it became impossible to escape, and resentment and fear surged through me with such terrifying force that I thought I'd drown. Finally, it spewed me out, leaving my mind and body utterly exhausted.

I was sick of all this. Sick of being tired. Sick of my mind racing round in circles. Sick of dreams where I was running for my life through knee-deep treacle.

What made it worse was that Stu had started coming round again asking to see me – trying to get me on my own. I'd managed to avoid being left with him, but every time the doorbell went I broke out in a sweat.

'Good grief!' I thought. 'I'm a nervous wreck.'

Covering my face with my arms, I closed my eyes and slipped into a weary doze – only to be jolted awake a few minutes later by a mighty commotion below.

Leaping downstairs, I arrived on the landing to find Adam cowering in the bathroom, ankle-deep in water, and Mum towering with rage in the doorway. The little wally had flushed the toilet – goodness knows why – and water was pouring over the rim like Niagara Falls, flooding the loo and spreading in a dark stain across the landing carpet.

We were still taking in the full horror of it when Gran screeched from below. 'Sylvia. *Sylvia!* There's water dripping from the electric light in the kitchen.'

'Gordon Bennett!' exploded Mum, dragging Adam out of the loo by his tee-shirt. Flattening us both against the wall, she raced to the stairs and leapt down them, three at a time, yelling for Dad.

Adam fled to the attic, sobbing and terrified, but I followed Mum to the kitchen where Grandma was dithering about, trying to catch water from the light in the washing-up bowl.

'Give me that,' said Mum, grabbing it out of her hands.

Without thinking, I reached over to the light switch.

'No! Don't touch,' she yelled. 'You'll electrocute yourself!'

Dad burst in from the shop. 'What the . . . ?'

'Turn off the electricity!' ordered Mum. 'There's been a flood.'

Dad disappeared, and a few seconds later everything electrical went off.

'What's going on?' he demanded, reappearing in the doorway.

'Your precious son flushed Adam's blanket down the loo, and it's blocked it and caused a flood.'

'Hey! That's not fair,' I protested. 'He started it – he ripped up my . . . .'

'We've had just about enough from you, Darrel,' snapped Dad, grabbing a bucket and floorcloth before heading hotfoot for the stairs. 'You've been a little brute lately. Just get out of my sight.'

*　　　　*　　　　*

The dry, cracked surface of the cliff broke beneath my feet, disintegrating into a mass of soil and small stones which bounced down the steep slope to land on the rocks below. I slid uncontrollably for a few metres, grabbing handfuls of coarse grass to slow myself down, until I reached the spot where two buttresses of rock formed a wide, sheltered niche.

Glad to be alone, I flung myself down among the coltsfoot leaves and harebells, breathing in the faint honey scent of the grass.

The niche was hidden on three sides, but open to the sea, and Stu and I had spent whole days there, playing hide-and-seek among the the rocks and feeding our fire with driftwood.

When it was wet we'd hid in caves formed by the angles of the rocks. In a real downpour, though, we'd made for the concrete pill-box on the headland – this whole coast was thick with wartime remains. But we'd never stayed in there long 'cos it was dank and smelly.

Today the weather was perfect, except for a cool breeze that sprang up towards late afternoon. But I couldn't enjoy it. I just felt so – so depressed.

The shadows were getting long, and I was just thinking of moving when a sudden shower of stones warned me that someone else was making the steep descent into the bay.

I worked myself backwards, deeper into the plants, hoping not to be noticed as the intruder crossed in front of my hiding-place. The cool, flat leaves of the coltsfoot brushed my face as I waited, and I could see tiny snails curled in the axils of the leaves.

But the footsteps didn't pass. They stopped on the smooth, iron-stained rocks just at the foot of the cleft. Curious, I craned my head forward and peered down – and instantly wished I hadn't. It was Stu standing there, dressed in his jeans and Chicago Bears sweatshirt and shading his eyes against the setting sun.

Guiltily I scrambled up, brushing soil off my trousers.

'I'm just off home,' I said tersely. 'What do you want?'

'I found your bike in the brambles up there.' He jerked his head in the direction of the cliff top. 'I just wanted to talk to you, that's all.'

I stuck my hands in my pockets and scowled at him unhelpfully. 'So?'

'I haven't really seen you since that day in town . . . .'

'You mean the day you pinched those shades?' I said nastily.

'Yeah, well – that's what I want to talk about.'

'What's there to say?' I asked, stepping smartly round him and heading off up the cliff. 'It's nothing to do with me.'

He scrambled after me, trainers slipping on the loose, dry surface. 'That's just it, Daz,' he insisted. 'I think it's got everything to do with you.'

My stomach did a somersault. I had to get away! I speeded up, breath rasping, legs aching, trying to put some distance between us.

From the top of the cliff it took only a moment to cross the coastal path and drop down to where I'd hidden my bike. But the flaming thing had got stuck in the brambles, and I was still struggling with it when Stu caught up with me and stood balanced unevenly on the steep path, blocking my escape.

'It was you, wasn't it, Daz?' he challenged. 'You put

those shades in my bag.'

'You're round the bend,' I snapped, dragging my bike free with mounting panic. 'You're the one they collared, and you don't have a scrap of evidence . . . .'

'No, I don't – but I've thought about it a lot and I think I know the score. You're not avoiding me because you think I'm a thief, you're doing it 'cos you've got a guilty conscience.'

'That's a load of codswallop, Mitchell,' I growled, heaving my bike up the slope towards him, 'Shove over!'

He didn't move, so I rammed him with my wheel. His feet slid a bit on the dry slope, but he stood his ground.

'None of the others could've done it,' he persisted. 'They were always in front of me. But you – you were behind me near the stand, and at the checkout when Sully searched the others. I'm not sure when you did it. I just know you did.'

It's not clear what happened after that. I know I shoved him again to get him out of the way, but somehow we got tangled up – him, the bike and me – and I lost my footing. I think he tried to grab me, 'cos the next minute we were both plunging down the slope in a tangle of arms and legs and twisted metal.

I only had one arm free – the other one was trapped in the bike-frame – and I was grabbing at anything to try and stop our headlong descent towards the target bunkers.

The trouble was, the whole slope was a mass of brambles – that's what made it such a good cover for our hideout – so my hand was soon cut to shreds by the sharp thorns. I had to let go, and we tumbled unchecked over the edge of the concrete bunker.

As we fell, the bike caught on a root. My right arm, trapped between the wheel and the frame of the bike, gave a sharp 'Crack!' as the bone broke.

It was a terrifying moment – hurtling through the air, out of control. I hit the ground shoulder first, and massive bolts of pain shot up my arm, leaving me faint and sick.

Several minutes elapsed before I was able to lift my head and look round. Up above I could see my bike, one wheel stuck on the root, the other still spinning gently over the void.

Waves of pain broke over me as I inched into a position where I could look around the bunker.

'Stu!' I cried, *'Stu!'*

But the crumpled figure neither moved nor spoke.

14

The truth is out

I scanned Stu's body for signs of life, but found nothing.

Bubbles of pure panic burst in my mind as I dragged myself across the boulder-strewn floor towards him. Already my thoughts were leaping ahead as fear discharged its poison into my mind. I was sure he was dead, and *I'd* killed him!

As I got nearer I could see the pasty whiteness of his skin, the blood on the stone near his head, the unnatural angle of his left leg – the whole picture made infinitely worse by the long, blood-covered scratches on his face and hands from our headlong plunge through the brambles.

Already I could see my moment of confession and hear my voice cracking, 'Stuart's dead. And I killed him!'

It painted a lurid scene. Stu's parents weeping, mine outraged – all of them turning away from me with cold animosity.

'I'm sorry. Stu's dead – and it was my fault.'

My arm was agony, and the dirt-filled scratches on my hands stung like fury. But I ignored them, worming my way across the floor of the bunker until an awkward movement sent an excruciating bolt of pain up to my shoulder, bringing me to a halt.

Fighting back waves of nausea I shut my eyes and waited

for them to subside.

It was my fault that Stu was lying there. The whole thing, from start to finish, was down to me. How had I got into this mess? Where had it begun?

I'd been a different person in Newton Bridge – easy-going, cheerful. What had happened to me? In a few short months I'd become a moody, friendless thief who'd ruined his best pal's life to save his own skin.

I moved again carefully, glad to find that the black spots weren't dancing in front of my eyes any more and that I didn't feel so sick. Holding my right arm as still as possible, I continued shuffling painfully towards Stu, edging round his twisted leg to where I could get a proper look at him.

'Stu?' I breathed, scanning the white face, fearful of touching him, afraid that my worst forebodings might actually be true. 'Stu?'

If only I had a mirror to put in front of his lips. In films they often use a mirror to see whether someone's still breathing. Maybe I could find a bit of glass – even reach the mirror on my bike. Slim chance really, but I had to try.

The faint breath of sound escaping from Stu's lips was so quiet I almost missed it, but my eyes caught the slight tremor as his eyelids flickered.

'Stu!' I pleaded, getting as close as I dared.

He stirred slightly, opening his eyes with an effort.

'Daz? What happened?'

'We fell into the den. Your leg's broken – so's my arm, I think. It hurts like heck, anyway. But for a minute I thought you were dead.'

He shut his eyes again, and I watched the pulse beating light and fast in his neck. He was sweating, too, so I tried to undo the top button of his shirt. It was difficult to manage with only one hand – but where my fingers touched his skin it felt cold and clammy and faintly greasy from the sheen of sweat.

He was showing all the signs of shock, and I racked my brain trying to remember what we'd been taught to do about it in first-aid.

Stu slowly licked his dry lips. 'I could do with a drink,' he murmured.

'Right on!' I said, glad to have something I could do.

My water-bottle had come loose in the crash and I'd seen it lying on the ground under the bike, so I wormed my way over.

I was just congratulating myself on having bought the flip-top type – easily opened by one hand and a set of teeth – when it all came back to me. No drinks, no food – especially if there was a chance that there were broken bones. It was something to do with anaesthetics – I'd forgotten the details – but it meant that a drink was out.

'Just *great*,' I sighed, wondering what to do next. It's OK messing about with first-aid when nobody's really hurt and you've got all the right gear. Me and Ranjit had had a good laugh fixing Dave up like Tutankhamen. But this was the real thing, and I'd no equipment and only one good arm.

I'd never felt less like laughing in my whole life.

I shuffled back. 'Can't give you a drink 'cos you might have to have an anaesthetic later on when they set your leg,' I explained, tearing the top off the bottle with my teeth and pouring a little water on to my almost-clean hanky. 'But this'll just wet your lips a bit.'

After that there wasn't much else I could do. I didn't have anything to cover him with, and I couldn't have moved him even if I'd wanted to. So I just got down to some serious worry.

What if nobody found us? Mum and Dad might know I was on the cliffs – but which cliffs? And where? They wouldn't have a clue. And what if Stu had done more than just break his leg? He'd been out cold for a bit, and there was all that blood on the stone near his head.

'Stu – does anyone know you're here?'

'Mmm?'

'Did you tell anyone you were coming to the cliffs?'

I could see his brain ticking over sluggishly as he thought about it.

'No,' he said finally. 'But I've asked God to tell my dad where we are.'

That seemed a brainless sort of attitude to me – even making allowances for the bang on the head.

'But your dad won't know to come here,' I argued. 'We agreed not to tell him about this den.'

'I know – and I didn't tell 'cos it was our secret. But Dad knows this cliff like the back of his hand – he'll remember this place and come looking.'

'I wish I had your faith,' I retorted, with a bitterness that I hadn't intended.

'I wish you had, too,' he said, shutting his eyes again.

It was quite dark now, but I could still make out the awful colour of his skin and hear his shallow, painful breathing. He needed help – and fast.

'Maybe he's not so daft,' I thought. 'Maybe I should pray, too. But I can't, 'cos it's my fault we're here.'

I shuffled sideways so that I could rest my back against the wall. Pain was making me feel sick again, but I breathed deeply, and after a minute or two it went off. But in that couple of minutes my decision was made.

'Stu?' I faltered, 'Can you hear me? I've got to tell you something.'

He didn't speak, and his face was just a pale glimmer in the dark as I began my confession.

'All that stuff you said before we fell – about the shades and all – well, you were right.'

He was so quiet that at first I didn't think he'd heard, but then he released his breath in a long sigh, as though he'd been holding it while I spoke.

'You were right about Simon and the gang, too. They stole anything they could lay their hands on – from shops, from kids at school – anything.'

There was a pause.

'And so did I. In fact, I was one of the worst.'

Stu lay there saying nothing as layer by layer I peeled back the pretence, exposing all the wrong choices, all the bitterness, all the secret, shameful things I'd done.

'So I just panicked and dropped them in your bag, never thinking that Sully would search you. I'm sorry for what I've done, and when we get out of this I'm going to go to the police and tell them the lot.'

What more could I say to him? Every word of my confession had driven the wedge deeper into the split. There couldn't be anything left between us now – he was so transparently honest, while I was up to the neck in theft and lies. I'd never wanted or needed his friendship more than I did right then. But it was too late – all I could do now was clear his name.

Confessing everything had left me feeling hollow and scoured out. But already, bad conscience was creeping back into the empty space – and I knew that admitting the truth to Stu wasn't enough. I still wasn't free, but what else could I do?

'Thanks for telling me, Daz,' said Stu, his voice warm and steady in the darkness. 'I forgive you – no problem.'

I waited, bracing myself for the brush-off. But it never came. He couldn't just forgive me like that – there had to be a snag!

'There's one thing, though.'

My heart nose-dived into my boots. Of course there was a snag. Stupid of me to imagine that things could ever be OK between us.

'You and me – we can forget all this now and still be

friends, but . . . .'

I looked up, trying to see his face through the darkness.

'. . . no matter what you do to put things right, you'll never get clear of the bad feelings inside until you get God's forgiveness, too.'

There was a long silence.

'Daz?'

'Yeah, I hear you.'

'That's who you've been running away from all this time. Not me, or your dad, or anybody else – only God. But there's nowhere you can hide 'cos he's always there with you, wherever you go. If you stop running and face up to things and ask him to forgive you, he'll do it straightaway. Then he'll stop you hurting inside – 'cos he loves you.'

Was I glad then that we couldn't see each other! I was having a bad time trying to keep a grip on things.

I'd prided myself on being too cool to need God. Now, suddenly, everything Stu was saying was falling into place.

'But, Stu,' I answered in a shaky voice, 'I don't even know where to begin.'

'No sweat, pal. You're on your way already.'

15

Rescue!

I learned a lot about Stu that night. He told me things about himself that I'd never heard before – probably 'cos I'd never let him get within a mile of telling me – and I knew that we were better friends now than we'd ever been.

He talked about God and Jesus just like they were there with us. But this time it didn't sound weird to me.

The only misgiving I had was whether Stu was right about God's wanting to forgive me. After all, Stu was the sort who thought riding his bike on the pavement was a major crime!

'What if God doesn't want to know?' I asked. 'I mean, what I've been doing really stinks.'

'God doesn't grade sins on a scale of one to ten like we do,' he explained. 'You know, ten out of ten for mass murder and one out of ten for a rude word. It's all just *sin* to him, and he hates it, whatever it is.'

Stu told me that Jesus died to pay for everything, and God would forgive it all if I asked him.

This all sounds very cosy until you remember that it was past eleven o'clock at night and we were stuck miles from anywhere, three metres down in a concrete pit, with at least two broken limbs and several other unidentified injuries.

Stu was desperately in need of help now – shivering uncontrollably and very weak – and I was in helpless agony

with my arm. But the fact that Stu was my friend again
blasted a shot of pure confidence through my veins, and his
statement about God telling his dad we were here didn't seem
so crazy after all.

There was no way I could have slept – my arm felt like
it was on fire – but I must have dozed a bit 'cos I nearly
missed seeing the torches as they bobbed along the top of the
cliff. In my half-awake state they just looked like two rather
active stars among millions of others.

'D-a-r-r-e-l!'

The voice carried over the still night air, and I struggled
into a sitting position, not sure if I was dreaming. I strained
to listen, but all I could hear was the sound of waves breaking
on the rocks down in the bay.

Had I imagined it after all?

'St-u-a-r-t!'

Shaking with relief I recognised Ted's voice and yelled,
'Down here – in the target bunker.'

Grit showered on us as our invisible rescuers slid down the
slope, torches dancing crazily as they skidded on the path.

Light flashed on the chrome bars of my bike and stopped
there. The beam of the torch moved over the twisted frame
until, with a sharp exclamation, our rescuers saw the front
wheel hooked precariously over the root and the rest of the
bike dangling over the dark void.

Then the light slid down the side of the bunker and within
seconds we were shielding our eyes from the glare.

'Thank God, they're here.'

Ted dropped the last few feet and hurried over, crouching
to examine our injuries with his torch. A couple of seconds
later there was another thud. This time it was Dad who
appeared out of the murk, his face tight with anxiety.

It's hard to put into words what it was like to see him again
without sounding like a real wally – but it was pretty
emotional, I can tell you. And if I'd had two good arms I'd

have hugged him to death.

'Stu's in a bad way, Dad,' I said urgently when things calmed down a bit. 'He got a bang on the head as well as that broken leg. He was out cold for a few minutes.'

Ted examined Stu's head carefully.

'I think the blood's from a cut by his ear and not serious, but if he was unconscious it'll need an X-ray to make sure he's OK.'

They debated for a bit, deciding who was going to do what – and in the end Ted went hurrying back for help on the grounds that he knew the area even in the dark. If Dad had gone he'd probably have walked off the edge of the cliff and we'd never have seen him again!

Dad covered a now dozing Stu with Ted's coat, then carefully tucked his own round me. Next, he went round the bunker collecting twigs and chunks of wood and lit a fire. In a few minutes, warmth was seeping back into my chilled body.

We sat together in the glow, watching the flames lick round the burning branches. Dad poked the fire with a stick.

'That was good thinking, remembering what they'd said in first-aid about drinks and food – but I'll bet you're starving. When this is sorted out,' – he pointed to my arm – 'I'll cook you up a feast.'

'Bacon, egg, fried bread, beans,' I drooled. 'You're on!'

We grinned at each other in the flickering light. Something had changed. Was it me?

My heart started pounding as I realised I'd got to tell him what had really been happening. But what would he say? What if he . . . ?

'Dad.'

'Mmm? What?'

I thought it would be easier telling it all the second time around – but it wasn't. I told him how it started back in Newton Bridge, about Si and the arcades, the shop-lifting,

Stu and the sunglasses and finally our fight on the cliff.

Every so often he'd cover his face and say, 'My God,' in a horrified whisper.

When I explained what I wanted to do to put it right, he heaved a long sigh, his eyes sparkling with tears in the firelight.

'God help us, Darrel,' he groaned. 'We've made a mess of this, haven't we?'

He stared into the fire again.

'I'm sorry, son. I never realised what was going on – how you were feeling. No, that's not true – I did see, but I was just too busy . . . .'

'Dad, how did you find us?' I asked, relieved to change the subject.

'Stu called round when his club finished,' he answered.

He threw another chunk of wood on the fire, sending a shower of sparks flying into the air.

'I told him you'd gone off in a huff, and he volunteered to find you. Even when it got late I wasn't too worried, 'cos you and Stu were always sensible. But when neither of you turned up at bedtime – that was different.

'Some kid told Ted that Stuart had gone to the beach, so we headed down there and searched right along. Not a sign. We worked our way across the rocks round into – what do you call this place – Jackson's Bay?'

I nodded.

'We were shouting all the time. Didn't you hear us?'

'No, not a thing. These concrete walls kill the sound.'

Dad poked the fire and rearranged the coat over Stu's legs.

'We got right on to that old pill-box before the tide stopped us. By that time we were stumped where to look next, so we sat down while Ted had a think. No point in my doing anything – I was totally lost anyway.

'Ted tried to ease the tension by telling me how he'd taken Stuart all over these cliffs, and how he'd explored them with his own dad back in the fifties. Stu's grandad had been in the Home Guard for part of the war, building pill-boxes up the coast and lighting fires on the moors to fool the German bombers – things like that.

'It was when he was talking about field-gun practice on the cliffs that Ted yelled *'Got it!'* so loud that I nearly fell off my rock.

'He charged off up the cliff, rabbiting on about a bunker where they kept the targets.'

Dad looked round at our concrete hideout.

'So this is it. Apparently a couple of soldiers sat in this place winching the targets up and down and checking the accuracy of the firing.

'You can still see where the winching mechanism used to be,' he continued, pointing through the gloom to the rusting remains of ironwork in the wall. 'And the grooves worn by the sliding trap-doors. Ted'd forgotten ever telling Stuart about it. Good job he remembered when he did.'

'Yeah,' I agreed thankfully. Then I recalled how the delay gave time for me and Stu to get our friendship sorted out – and even for me to find the answer to what I was looking for.

Lights appeared on the cliff-top and the sound of sliding feet and urgent voices wafted down to our make-shift camp.

Stu stirred painfully.

'Brian,' he said to my dad, 'will Daz be OK? I mean about the shop-lifting and all that?'

Dad looked at me, his eyes troubled.

'It's not going to be easy for him, Stuart, and that's a fact.

'But he's got us with him all the way, hasn't he? He'll be all right. You'll see.'